FRANCESCA SIMON

THE BiG BOOK OF HORRiD HENRY

Illustrated by
Tony Ross

Orion
Children's Books

First published in Great Britain in 2006 and 2007 as
Horrid Henry's Evil Enemies and *Horrid Henry Rules the World*
by Orion Children's Books
a division of the Orion Publishing Group Ltd
Orion House
5 Upper Saint Martin's Lane
London WC2H 9EA

ISBN 978 1 40723 950 7

Printed in China

CONTENTS

THE USUAL SUSPECTS

HORRID HENRY
AND
MOODY MARGARET

'I'm Captain Hook!'

'No, I'm Captain Hook!'

'I'm Captain Hook,' said Horrid Henry.

'I'm Captain Hook,' said Moody Margaret.

They glared at each other.

'It's *my* hook,' said Moody Margaret.

Moody Margaret lived next door. She did not like Horrid Henry, and Horrid Henry did not like her. But when Rude Ralph was busy, Clever Clare had flu, and Sour Susan was her enemy, Margaret would jump over the wall to play with Henry.

'Actually, it's my turn to be Hook now,' said Perfect Peter. 'I've been the prisoner for such a long time.'

'Prisoner, be quiet!' said Henry.

'Prisoner, walk the plank!' said Margaret.

'But I've walked it fourteen times already,' said Peter. 'Please can I be Hook now?'

'No, by thunder!' said Moody Margaret. 'Now out of my way, worm!' And she swashbuckled across the desk, waving her hook and clutching her sword and dagger.

Margaret had eyepatches and skulls and crossbones and plumed hats and cutlasses and sabres and snickersnees.

Henry had a stick.

This was why Henry played with Margaret.

But Henry had to do terrible things before playing with Margaret's swords. Sometimes he had to sit and wait while she read a book. Sometimes he had to play 'Mums and Dads' with her. Worst of all (please don't tell anyone), sometimes he had to be the baby.

Henry never knew what Margaret would do.

When he put a spider on her arm, Margaret laughed.

When he pulled her hair, Margaret pulled his harder.

When Henry screamed, Margaret would scream louder. Or she would sing. Or pretend not to hear.

Sometimes Margaret was fun. But most of the time she was a moody old grouch.

'I won't play if I can't be Hook,' said Horrid Henry.

Margaret thought for a moment.

'We can both be Captain Hook,' she said.

'But we only have one hook,' said Henry.

'Which I haven't played with yet,' said Peter.

'BE QUIET, prisoner!' shouted Margaret. 'Mr Smee, take him to jail.'

'No,' said Henry.

'You will get your reward, Mr Smee,' said the Captain, waving her hook.

Mr Smee dragged the prisoner to the jail.

'If you're very quiet, prisoner, then you will be freed and you can be a pirate, too,' said Captain Hook.

'Now give me the hook,' said Mr Smee.
The Captain reluctantly handed it over.
'Now I'm Captain Hook and you're Mr Smee,' shouted Henry. 'I order everyone to walk the plank!'
'I'm sick of playing pirates,' said Margaret. 'Let's

play something else.'

Henry was furious. That
was just like Moody Margaret.

'Well, I'm playing pirates,'
said Henry.

'Well I'm not,' said
Margaret. 'Give me back my
hook.'

'No,' said Henry.

Moody Margaret opened
her mouth and screamed. Once
Margaret started screaming she could go on and on
and on.

Henry gave her the hook.

Margaret smiled.

'I'm hungry,' she said.
'Got anything good to
eat?'

Henry had three bags of
crisps and seven chocolate
biscuits hidden in his
room, but he certainly
wasn't going to share
them with Margaret.

'You can have a radish,'
said Henry.

'What else?' said Margaret.

'A carrot,' said Henry.

'What else?' said Margaret.

'Glop,' said Henry.

'What's Glop?'

'Something special that only I can make,' said Henry.

'What's in it?' asked Margaret.

'That's a secret,' said Henry.

'I bet it's yucky,' said Margaret.

'Of course it's yucky.' said Henry.

'I can make the yuckiest Glop of all,' said Margaret.

'That's because you don't know anything. No one can make yuckier Glop than I can.'

'I dare you to eat Glop,' said Margaret.

'I double dare you back,' said Henry. 'Dares go first.'

Margaret stood up very straight.

'All right,' said Margaret. 'Glop starts with snails and worms.'

And she started poking under the bushes.

'Got one!' she shouted, holding up a fat snail.

'Now for some worms,' said Margaret.

She got down on her hands and knees and started digging a hole.

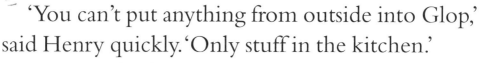

'You can't put anything from outside into Glop,' said Henry quickly. 'Only stuff in the kitchen.'

Margaret looked at Henry.

'I thought we were making Glop,' she said.

'We are,' said Henry. 'My way, because it's *my* house.'

Horrid Henry and Moody Margaret went into the gleaming white kitchen. Henry got out two wooden mixing spoons and a giant red bowl.

'I'll start,' said Henry. He went to the cupboard and opened the doors wide.

'Porridge!' said Henry. And he poured some into the bowl.

Margaret opened the fridge and looked inside. She grabbed a small container.

'Soggy semolina!' shouted Margaret. Into the bowl it went.

'Coleslaw!'

'Spinach!'

'Coffee!'

'Yoghurt!'

'Flour!'

'Vinegar!'

'Baked beans!'

'Mustard!'

'Peanut butter!'

'Mouldy cheese!'

'Pepper!'

'Rotten oranges!'

'And ketchup!' shouted Henry.

He squirted in the ketchup until the bottle was empty.

'Now, mix!' said Margaret.

Horrid Henry and Moody Margaret grabbed hold of their spoons with both hands. Then they plunged the spoons into the Glop and began to stir.

It was hard heavy work.

Faster and faster, harder and harder they stirred.

There was Glop on the ceiling. There was Glop on the floor. There was Glop on the clock, and Glop on the door. Margaret's hair was covered in Glop. So was Henry's face.

Margaret looked into the bowl. She had never seen anything so yucky in her life.

'It's ready,' she said.

Horrid Henry and Moody Margaret carried the Glop to the table.

Then they sat down and stared at the sloppy, slimy, sludgy, sticky, smelly, gooey, gluey, gummy, greasy, gloopy Glop.

'Right,' said Henry. 'Who's going to eat some first?'

There was a very long pause.

Henry looked at Margaret.

Margaret looked at Henry.

'Me,' said Margaret. 'I'm not scared.'

She scooped up a large spoonful and stuffed it in her mouth.

Then she swallowed. Her face went pink and purple and green.

'How does it taste?' said Henry.

'Good,' said Margaret, trying not to choke.

'Have some more then,' said Henry.

'Your turn first,' said Margaret.

Henry sat for a moment and looked at the Glop.

'My mum doesn't like me to eat between meals,' said Henry.

'HENRY!' hissed Moody Margaret.

Henry took a tiny spoonful.

'More!' said Margaret.

Henry took a tiny bit more. The Glop wobbled lumpily on his spoon. It looked like . . . Henry did not want to think about what it looked like.

He closed his eyes and brought the spoon to his mouth.

'Ummm, yummm,' said Henry.

'You didn't eat any,' said Margaret. 'That's not fair.'

She scooped up some Glop and . . .

I dread to think what would have happened next, if they had not been interrupted.

'Can I come out now?' called a small voice from outside. 'It's my turn to be Hook.'

Horrid Henry had forgotten all about Perfect Peter.

'OK,' shouted Henry.

Peter came to the door.

'I'm hungry,' he said.

'Come in, Peter,' said Henry sweetly. 'Your dinner is on the table.'

SPECIAL GLOP RECIPES

Wormy Glop

Worms
Beetroot
Mud
Vinegar
Salt

Rotten Glop

Banana **peel**
Rotten lemons
Cold porridge
Horseradish
Cola

Toothpaste Glop

Lumpy custard
Brussels sprouts
peelings
Toothpaste
Yoghurt
Mustard

HORRID HENRY'S TOP SECRET UNBREAKABLE CODE

A = Z	J = Q	S = H
B = Y	K = P	T = G
C = X	L = O	U = F
D = W	M = N	V = E
E = V	N = M	W = D
F = U	O = L	X = C
G = T	P = K	Y = B
H = S	Q = J	Z = A
I = R	R = I	

HNVOOB TLZW YILGSVIH PVVK LFG.

WARNING:

DO NOT LOOK on page 164!

HORRID HENRY AND THE SECRET CLUB

'**H**alt! Who goes there?'

'Me.'

'Who's me?' said Moody Margaret.

'ME!' said Sour Susan.

'What's the password?'

'Uhhhh . . .' Sour Susan paused. What was the password? She thought and thought and thought.

'Potatoes?'

Margaret sighed loudly. Why was she friends with such a stupid person?

'No it isn't.'

'Yes it is,' said Susan.

'Potatoes was last week's password,' said Margaret.

'No it wasn't.'

'Yes it was,' said Moody Margaret. 'It's my club and I decide.'

There was a long pause.

'All right,' said Susan sourly. 'What *is* the password?'

'I don't know if I'm going to tell you,' said Margaret. 'I could be giving away a big secret to the enemy.'

'But I'm not the enemy,' said Susan. 'I'm Susan.'

'Shhhh!' said Margaret. 'We don't want Henry to find out who's in the secret club.'

Susan looked quickly over her shoulder. The enemy was nowhere to be seen. She whistled twice.

'All clear,' said Sour Susan. 'Now let me in.'

Moody Margaret thought for a moment. Letting someone in without the password broke the first club rule.

'Prove to me you're Susan, and not the enemy pretending to be Susan,' said Margaret.

'You know it's me,' wailed Susan.

'Prove it.'

Susan stuck her foot into the tent.

'I'm wearing the black patent leather shoes with the blue flowers I always wear.'

'No good,' said Margaret. 'The enemy could have stolen them.'

'I'm speaking with Susan's voice and I look like Susan,' said Susan.

'No good,' said Margaret. 'The enemy could be a master of disguise.'

Susan stamped her foot. 'And I know that you were the one who pinched Helen and I'm going to tell Miss . . .'

'Come closer to the tent flap,' said Margaret.

Susan bent over.

'Now listen to me,' said Margaret. 'Because I'm only going to tell you once. When a secret club member wants to come in they say NUNGA. Anyone inside answers back, 'Nunga Nu.' That's how I know it's you and you know it's me.'

'NUNGA,' said Sour Susan.

'NUNGA NU,' said Moody Margaret. 'Enter.'

Susan entered the club. She gave the secret handshake, sat down on her box and sulked.

'You knew it was me all along,' said Susan.

Margaret scowled at her.

'That's not the point. If you don't want to obey the club rules you can leave.'

Susan didn't move.

'Can I have a biscuit?' she said.

Margaret smiled graciously. 'Have two,' she said. 'Then we'll get down to business.'

Meanwhile, hidden under a bush behind some strategically placed branches, another top secret meeting was taking place in the next door garden.

'I think that's everything,' said the Leader. 'I shall now put the plans into action.'

'What am I going to do?' said Perfect Peter.

'Stand guard,' said Horrid Henry.

'I always have to stand guard,' said Peter, as the Leader crept out.

'It's not fair.'

'Have you brought your spy report?' asked Margaret.

'Yes,' said Susan.

'Read it aloud,' said Margaret.

Susan took out a piece of paper and read:

'I watched the enemy's house for two hours yesterday morning –'

'Which morning?' interrupted Margaret.

'Saturday morning,' said Susan. 'A lady with grey

hair and a beret walked past.'

'What colour was the beret?' said Margaret.

'I don't know,' said Susan.

'Call yourself a spy and you don't know what colour the beret was,' said Margaret.

'Can I please continue with my report?' said Susan.

'I'm not stopping you,' said Margaret.

'Then I saw the enemy leave the house with his brother and mother. The enemy kicked his brother twice. His mother shouted at him. Then I saw the postman –'

'**NUNGA!**' screeched a voice from outside.

Margaret and Susan froze.

'**NUNGA!!!**' screeched the voice again. 'I know you're in there!'

27

'Aaaahh!' squeaked Susan. 'It's Henry!'

'Quick! Hide!' hissed Margaret.

The secret spies crouched behind two boxes.

'You told him our password!' hissed Margaret. 'How dare you!'

'Wasn't me!' hissed Susan. 'I couldn't even remember it, so how could I have told him? You told him!'

'Didn't,' hissed Margaret.

'NUNGA!!!' screeched Henry again. 'You have to let me in! I know the password.'

'What do we do?' hissed Susan. 'You said anyone who knows the password enters.'

'For the last time, NUNGAAAAA!' shouted Horrid Henry.

'Nunga Nu,' said Margaret. 'Enter.'

Henry swaggered into the tent. Margaret glared at him.

'Don't mind if I do,' said Henry, grabbing all the chocolate biscuits and stuffing them into his mouth. Then he sprawled on the rug, scattering crumbs everywhere.

'What are you doing?' said Horrid Henry.

'Nothing,' said Moody Margaret.

'Nothing,' said Sour Susan.

'You are, too,' said Henry.

'Mind your own business,' said Margaret. 'Now, Susan, let's vote on whether to allow boys in. I vote No.'

'I vote No, too,' said Susan.

'Sorry, Henry, you can't join. Now leave.'

'No,' said Henry.

'LEAVE,' said Margaret.

'Make me,' said Henry.

Margaret took a deep breath. Then she opened her mouth and screamed. No one could scream as loud, or as long, or as piercingly, as Moody Margaret. After a few moments, Susan started screaming too.

Henry got to his feet, knocking over the crate they used as a table.

'Watch out,' said Henry. 'Because the Purple Hand will be back!' He turned to go.

Moody Margaret sprang up behind him and pushed him through the flap. Henry landed in a heap outside.

'Can't get me!' shouted Henry. He picked himself up and jumped over the wall. 'The Purple Hand is the best!'

'Oh yeah,' muttered Margaret. 'We'll see about that.'

Henry checked over his shoulder to make sure no one was watching. Then he crept back to his fort.

'Smelly toads,' he whispered to the guard.

The branches parted. Henry climbed in.

'Did you attack them?' said Peter.

'Of course,' said Henry. 'Didn't you hear Margaret screaming?'

'I was the one who heard their password, so I think I should have gone,' said Peter.

'Whose club is this?' said Henry.

The corners of Peter's mouth began to turn down.

'Right, out!' said Henry.

'Sorry!' said Peter. 'Please, Henry, can I be a real member of the Purple Hand?'

'No,' said Henry. 'You're too young. And don't you dare come into the fort when I'm not here.'

'I won't,' said Peter.

'Good,' said Henry. 'Now here's the plan. I'm going to set a booby trap in Margaret's tent. Then when she goes in . . .' Henry shrieked with laughter as he pictured Moody Margaret covered in cold muddy water.

All was not well back at Moody Margaret's Secret Club.

'It's your fault,' said Margaret.

'It isn't,' said Susan.

'You're such a blabbermouth, and you're a terrible spy.'

'I am not,' said Susan.

'Well, I'm Leader, and I ban you from the club for a week for breaking our sacred rule and telling the enemy our password. Now go away.'

'Oh please let me stay,' said Susan.

'No,' said Margaret.

Susan knew there was no point arguing with Margaret when she got that horrible bossy look on her face.

'You're so mean,' said Susan.

Moody Margaret picked up a book and started to read.

Sour Susan got up and left.

'I know what I'll do to fix Henry,' thought Margaret. 'I'll set a booby trap in Henry's fort. Then when he goes in . . .' Margaret shrieked with laughter as she pictured Horrid Henry covered in cold muddy water.

Just before lunch Henry sneaked into Margaret's garden holding a plastic bucket of water and some string. He stretched the string just above the ground across the entrance and suspended the bucket above, with the other end of the string tied round it.

Just after lunch Margaret sneaked into Henry's garden holding a bucket of water and some string. She stretched the string across the fort's entrance and rigged up the bucket. What she wouldn't give to see Henry soaking wet when he tripped over the string and pulled the bucket of water down on him.

Perfect Peter came into the garden carrying a ball. Henry wouldn't play with him and there was nothing to do.

Why shouldn't I go into the fort? thought Peter. I helped build it.

Next door, Sour Susan slipped into the garden. She was feeling sulky.

Why shouldn't I go into the tent? thought Susan. It's my club too.

Perfect Peter walked into the fort and tripped.

CRASH! SPLASH!

Sour Susan walked into the tent and tripped.

CRASH! SPLASH!

Horrid Henry heard howls. He ran into the garden whooping.

'Ha! Ha! Margaret! Gotcha!'

Then he stopped.

Moody Margaret heard screams. She ran into the garden cheering.

'Ha! Ha! Henry! Gotcha!'

Then she stopped.

'That's it!' shrieked Peter. 'I'm leaving!'

'But it wasn't me,' said Henry.

'That's it!' sobbed Susan. 'I quit!'

'But it wasn't me,' said Margaret.

'Rats!' said Henry.

'Rats!' said Margaret.

They glared at each other.

EVIL ENEMY

Sour Susan

HFHZM SZH KLMT B KZMGH.

PURPLE HAND FORT

RULES

No girls allowed
Henry: Leader
Ralph: Deputy Leader
Peter: Sentry (junior)
Henry's Title: Lord High Excellent Majesty
Peters Title: Worm

Peter must bow to Henry and Ralph
Peter must never touch the purple hand skull and
        crossbones biscuit tin
Peter not allowed in the PurpleHand Fort
        without Henry's permission
Peter is a tempory member only.
Password: Smelly Toads
Motto: Down with girls

SECRET CLUB

Rules

No boys allowed
Margaret: Leader
Susan: Spy
Gurinder: biscuits and trainee spy
Linda: biscuits

Password: Nunga
Motto: Down with boys

HORRID HENRY'S CHRISTMAS

Perfect Peter sat on the sofa looking through the Toy Heaven catalogue. Henry had hogged it all morning to write his Christmas present list. Naturally, this was not a list of the presents Henry planned to give. This was a list of what he wanted to get.

Horrid Henry looked up from his work. He'd got a bit stuck after: a million pounds, a parrot, a machete, swimming pool, trampoline, and Killer Catapult.

'Gimme that!' shouted Horrid Henry. He snatched the Toy Heaven catalogue from Perfect Peter.

'You give that back!' shouted Peter.

'It's my turn!' shouted Henry.

'You've had it the whole morning!' shrieked Peter. 'Mum!'

'Stop being horrid, Henry,' said Mum, running in from the kitchen.

Henry ignored her. His eyes were glued to the catalogue. He'd found it. The toy of his dreams. The toy he had to have.

'I want a Boom-Boom Basher,' said Henry. It was a brilliant toy which crashed into everything, an ear-piercing siren wailing all the while. Plus all the trasher attachments. Just the thing for knocking down Perfect Peter's marble run.

'I've got to have a Boom-Boom Basher,' said Henry, adding it to his list in big letters.

'Absolutely not, Henry,' said Mum. 'I will not have that horrible noisy toy in my house.'

'Aw, come on,' said Henry. 'Pleeease.'

Dad came in.

'I want a Boom-Boom Basher for Christmas,' said Henry.

'No way,' said Dad. 'Too expensive.'

'You are the meanest, most horrible parents in the whole world,' screamed Henry. 'I hate you! I want a Boom-Boom Basher!'

'That's no way to ask, Henry,' said Perfect Peter. 'I want doesn't get.'

Henry lunged at Peter. He was an octopus squeezing the life out of the helpless fish trapped in its tentacles.

'Help,' spluttered Peter.

'Stop being horrid, Henry, or I'll cancel the visit to Father Christmas,' shouted Mum.

Henry stopped.

The smell of burning mince pies drifted into the room.

'Ahh, my pies!' shrieked Mum.

'How much longer are we going to have to wait?' whined Henry. 'I'm sick of this!'

Horrid Henry, Perfect Peter, and Mum were standing near the end of a very long queue waiting to see Father Christmas. They had been waiting for a very long time.

'Oh, Henry, isn't this exciting,' said Peter. 'A chance to meet Father Christmas. I don't mind how long I wait.'

'Well I do,' snapped Henry. He began to squirm his way through the crowd.

'Hey, stop pushing!' shouted Dizzy Dave.

'Wait your turn!' shouted Moody Margaret.

'I was here first!' shouted Lazy Linda.

Henry shoved his way in beside Rude Ralph.

'What are you asking Father Christmas for?' said Henry. 'I want a Boom-Boom Basher.'

'Me too,' said Ralph. 'And a Goo-Shooter.'

Henry's ears pricked up.

'What's that?'

'It's really cool,' said Ralph. 'It splatters green goo over everything and everybody.'

'Yeah!' said Horrid Henry as Mum dragged him back to his former place in the queue.

'What do you want for Christmas, Graham?' asked Santa.

'Sweets!' said Greedy Graham.

'What do you want for Christmas, Bert?' asked Santa.

'I dunno,' said Beefy Bert.

'What do you want for Christmas, Peter?' asked Santa.

'A dictionary!' said Peter. 'Stamps, seeds, a geometry kit, and some cello music, please.'

'No toys?'

'No thank you,' said Peter. 'I have plenty of toys already. Here's a present for you, Santa,' he added, holding out a beautifully wrapped package. 'I made it myself.'

'What a delightful young man,' said Santa. Mum beamed proudly.

'My turn now,' said Henry, pushing Peter off Santa's lap.

'And what do you want for Christmas, Henry?' asked Santa.

Henry unrolled the list.

'I want a Boom–Boom Basher and a Goo-Shooter,' said Henry.

'Well, we'll see about that,' said Santa.

'Great!' said Henry. When grown–ups said 'We'll see,' that almost always meant 'Yes.'

It was Christmas Eve.

Mum and Dad were rushing around the house tidying up as fast as they could.

Perfect Peter was watching a nature programme on TV.

'I want to watch cartoons!' said Henry. He grabbed the clicker and switched channels.

'I was watching the nature programme!' said Peter. 'Mum!'

'Stop it, Henry,' muttered Dad. 'Now, both of you, help tidy up before your aunt and cousin arrive.'

Perfect Peter jumped up to help.

Horrid Henry didn't move.

'Do they have to come?' said Henry.

'Yes,' said Mum.

'I hate cousin Steve,' said Henry.

'No you don't,' said Mum.

'I do too,' snarled Henry. If there was a yuckier person walking the earth than Stuck-up Steve, Henry had yet to meet him. It was the one bad thing about Christmas, having him come to stay every year.

Ding Dong. It must be Rich Aunt Ruby and his horrible cousin. Henry watched as his aunt staggered in carrying boxes and boxes of presents which she dropped under the brightly-lit tree. Most of them, no doubt, for Stuck-up Steve.

43

'I wish we weren't here,' moaned Stuck-up Steve. 'Our house is so much nicer.'

'Shh,' said Rich Aunt Ruby. She went off with Henry's parents.

Stuck-up Steve looked down at Henry.

'Bet I'll get loads more presents than you,' he said.

'Bet you won't,' said Henry, trying to sound convinced.

'It's not what you get it's the thought that counts,' said Perfect Peter.

'*I'm* getting a Boom-Boom Basher *and* a Goo-Shooter,' said Stuck-up Steve.

'So am I,' said Henry.

'Nah,' said Steve. 'You'll just get horrible presents like socks and stuff. And won't I laugh.'

When I'm king, thought Henry, I'll have a snake pit

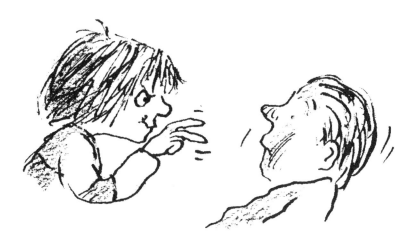

made just for Steve.

'I'm richer than you,' boasted Steve. 'And I've got loads more toys.' He looked at the Christmas tree.

'Call that twig a tree?' sneered Steve. 'Ours is so big it touches the ceiling.'

'Bedtime, boys,' called Dad. 'And remember, no one is to open any presents until we've eaten lunch and gone for a walk.'

'Good idea, Dad,' said Perfect Peter. 'It's always nice to have some fresh air on Christmas Day and leave the presents for later.'

Ha, thought Horrid Henry. We'll see about that.

The house was dark. The only noise was the rasping sound of Stuck-up Steve, snoring away in his sleeping bag.

Horrid Henry could not sleep. Was there a Boom-Boom Basher waiting for him downstairs?

He rolled over on his side and tried to get comfortable. It was no use. How could he live until Christmas morning?

Horrid Henry could bear it no longer. He had to find out if he'd been given a Boom-Boom Basher.

Henry crept out of bed, grabbed his torch, stepped over Stuck-up Steve – resisting the urge to stomp on him – and sneaked down the stairs.

CR-EEAK went the creaky stair. Henry froze. The house was silent.

Henry tiptoed into the dark sitting room. There was the tree. And there were all the presents, loads and

46

loads and loads of them!

Right, thought Henry, I'll just have a quick look for my Boom-Boom Basher and then get straight back to bed.

He seized a giant package. This looked promising. He gave it a shake. Thud-thud-thunk. This sounds good, thought Henry. His heart leapt. I just know it's a Boom-Boom Basher. Then he checked the label: 'Merry Christmas, Steve.'

Rats, thought Henry.

He shook another temptingly-shaped present: 'Merry Christmas, Steve.' And another: 'Merry Christmas, Steve.' And another. And another.

Then Henry felt a small, soft, squishy package. Socks for sure. I hope it's not for me, he thought. He checked the label: 'Merry Christmas, Henry.'

There must be some mistake, thought Henry. Steve needs socks more than I do. In fact, I'd be doing him a favour giving them to him.

Switch! It was the work of a moment to swap labels.

Now, let's see, thought Henry. He eyed a Goo-Shooter shaped package with Steve's name on it, then found another, definitely book-shaped one, intended for himself.

Switch!

Come to think of it, Steve had far too many toys

cluttering up his house. Henry had heard Aunt Ruby complaining about the mess just tonight.

Switch! Switch! Switch! Then Horrid Henry crept back to bed.

It was 6:00 a.m.

'Merry Christmas!' shouted Henry. 'Time to open the presents!'

Before anyone could stop him Henry thundered downstairs.

Stuck-up Steve jumped up and followed him.

'Wait!' shouted Mum.

'Wait!' shouted Dad.

The boys dashed into the sitting room and flung themselves upon the presents. The room was filled with shrieks of delight and howls of dismay as they tore off the wrapping paper.

'Socks!' screamed Stuck-up Steve. 'What a crummy present! Thanks for nothing!'

'Don't be so rude, Steve,' said Rich Aunt Ruby, yawning.

'A Goo-Shooter!' shouted Horrid Henry. 'Wow! Just what I wanted!'

'A geometry set,' said Perfect Peter. 'Great!'

'A flower-growing kit?' howled Stuck-up Steve. 'Phooey!'

'Make Your Own Fireworks!' beamed Henry. 'Wow!'

'Tangerines!' screamed Stuck-up Steve. 'This is the worst Christmas ever!'

'A Boom-Boom Basher!' beamed Henry. 'Gee, thanks. Just what I wanted!'

'Let me see that label,' snarled Steve. He grabbed the torn wrapping paper. 'Merry Christmas, Henry,' read the label. There was no mistake.

'Where's *my* Boom–Boom Basher?' screamed Steve.

'It must be here somewhere,' said Aunt Ruby.

'Ruby, you shouldn't have bought one for Henry,' said Mum, frowning.

'I didn't,' said Ruby.

Mum looked at Dad.

'Nor me,' said Dad.

'Nor me,' said Mum.

'Father Christmas gave it to me,' said Horrid Henry. 'I asked him to and he did.'

Silence.

'He's got my presents!' screamed Steve. 'I want them back!'

'They're mine!' screamed Henry, clutching his booty. 'Father Christmas gave them to me.'

'No, mine!' screamed Steve.

Aunt Ruby inspected the labels. Then she looked grimly at the two howling boys.

'Perhaps I made a mistake when I labelled some of the presents,' she muttered to Mum. 'Never mind. We'll sort it out later,' she said to Steve.

'It's not fair!' howled Steve.

'Why don't you try on your new socks?' said Horrid Henry.

Stuck-up Steve lunged at Henry. But Henry was ready for him.

SPLAT!

'Aaaarggh!' screamed Steve, green goo dripping from his face and clothes and hair.

'HENRY!' screamed Mum and Dad. 'How could you be so horrid!'

'Boom–Boom

CRASH!
NEE NAW NEE NAW
WHOO WHOOO WHOOO!'

What a great Christmas, thought Henry, as his Boom–Boom Basher knocked over Peter's marble run.

'Say goodbye to Aunt Ruby, Henry,' said Mum. She looked tired.

Rich Aunt Ruby and Steve had decided to leave a little earlier than planned.

'Goodbye, Aunt,' said Henry. 'Goodbye, Steve. Can't wait to see you next Christmas.'

'Actually,' said Mum, 'you're staying the night next month.'

Uh-oh, thought Horrid Henry.

EVIL ENEMY

Stuck-up
Steve

R DZMG Z PROOVI XZGZKFOG ZMW YLLN-YLLN YZHSVI.

Dear Henry
Thank you for the socks and
tangerines (not)
Steve.

P.S. My mum made me write this.

Dear Steve
Wow! Thank you so
MUCH
for the Boom-Boom Basher
and Goo Shooter!
I think of you every time
I play with them!!!
What GREAT presents!
Hard luck you got socks.
Henry

HGVEV RH HGFXP-FK, BFXPB ZMW SLIIRYOV.

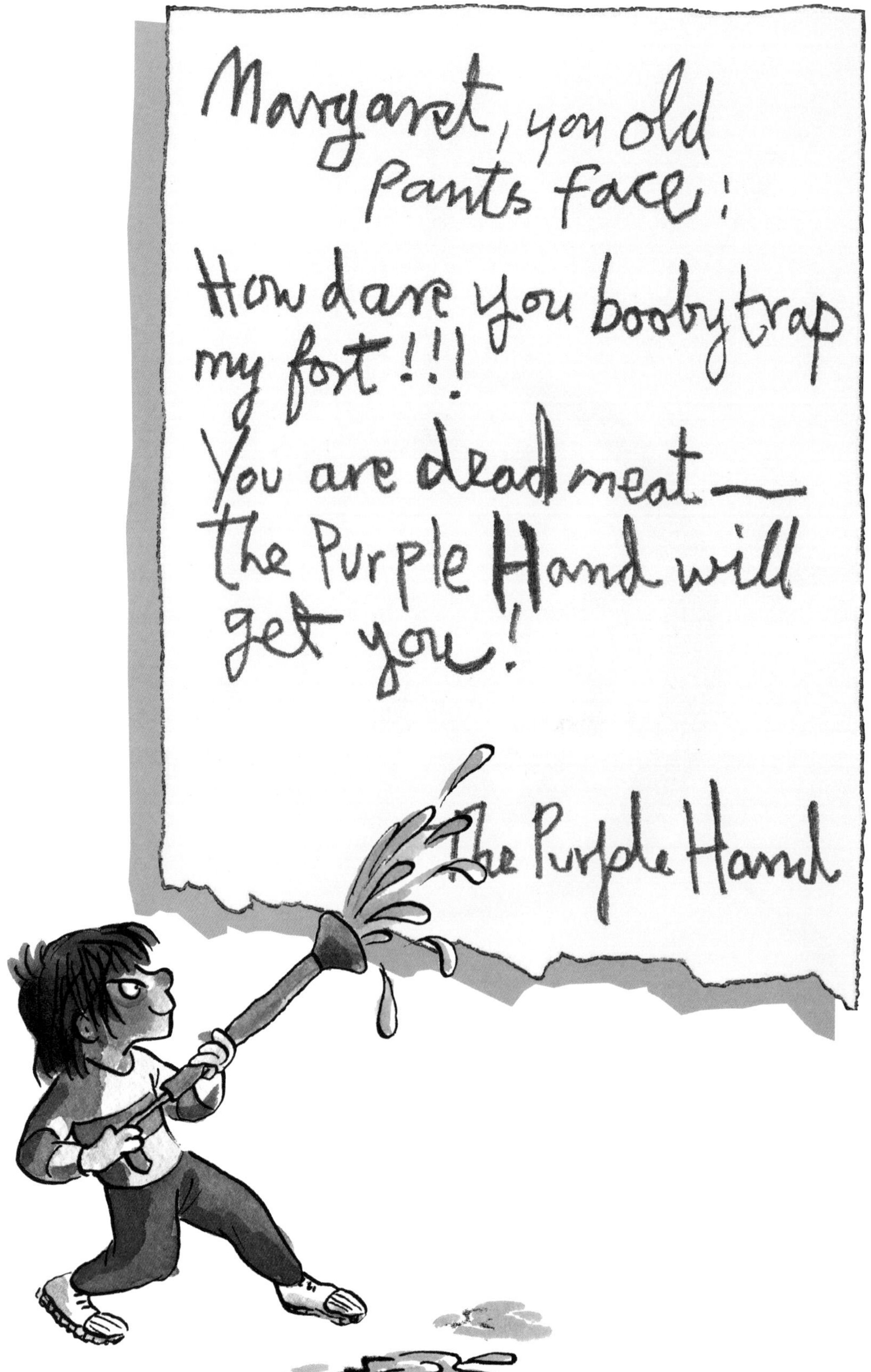
Margaret, you old
Pants face:
How dare you booby trap
my fort!!!
You are dead meat —
the Purple Hand will
get you!
The Purple Hand

HORRID HENRY'S HAUNTED HOUSE

'No way!' shrieked Horrid Henry. He was not staying the weekend with his slimy cousin Stuck-up Steve, and that was that. He sat in the back seat of the car with his arms folded.

'Yes you are,' said Mum.

'Steve can't wait to see you,' said Dad.

This was not exactly true. After Henry had sprayed Steve with green goo last Christmas, *and* helped himself to a few of Steve's presents, Steve had sworn revenge. Under the circumstances, Henry thought it would be a good idea to keep out of Steve's way.

And now Mum had arranged for him to spend the weekend while she and Dad went off on their own! Perfect Peter was staying with Tidy Ted, and he was stuck with Steve.

'It's a great chance for you boys to become good friends,' she said. 'Steve is a very nice boy.'

'I feel sick,' said Henry, coughing.

'Stop faking,' said Mum. 'You were well enough to play football all morning.'

'I'm too tired,' said Henry, yawning.

'I'm sure you'll get plenty of rest at Aunt Ruby's,' said Dad firmly.

'I'M NOT GOING!' howled Henry.

Mum and Dad took Henry by the arms, dragged him to Rich Aunt Ruby's door, and rang the bell.

The massive door opened immediately.

'Welcome, Henry,' said Rich Aunt Ruby, giving him a great smacking kiss.

'Henry, how lovely to see you,' said Stuck-up Steve sweetly. 'That's a very nice second-hand jumper you're wearing.'

'Hush, Steve,' said Rich Aunt Ruby. 'I think Henry looks very smart.'

Henry glared at Steve. Thank goodness he'd remembered his Goo-Shooter. He had a feeling he might need it.

'Goodbye, Henry,' said Mum. 'Be good. Ruby, thank you so much for having him.'

'Our pleasure,' lied Aunt Ruby.

The great door closed.

Henry was alone in the house with his arch-enemy.

Henry looked grimly at Steve. What a horrible boy, he thought.

Steve looked grimly at Henry. What a horrible boy, he thought.

'Why don't you both go upstairs and play in Steve's room till supper's ready?' said Aunt Ruby.

'I'll show Henry where he's sleeping first,' said Steve.

'Good idea,' said Aunt Ruby.

Reluctantly, Henry followed his cousin up the wide staircase.

'I bet you're scared of the dark,' said Steve.

''Course I'm not,' said Henry.

'That's good,' said Steve. 'This is my room,' he added, opening the door to an enormous bedroom. Horrid Henry stared longingly at the shelves filled to bursting with zillions of toys and games.

'Of course all *my* toys are brand new. Don't you dare touch anything,' hissed Steve. 'They're all mine and only *I* can play with them.'

Henry scowled. When he was king he'd use Steve's head for target practice.

They continued all the way to the top. Goodness, this old house was big, thought Henry.

Steve opened the door to a large attic bedroom, with brand new pink and blue flowered wallpaper, a four-poster bed, an enormous polished wood wardrobe, and two large windows.

'You're in the haunted room,' said Steve casually.

'Great!' said Henry. 'I love ghosts.' It would take more than a silly ghost to frighten *him*.

'Don't believe me if you don't want to,' said Steve. 'Just don't blame me when the ghost starts wailing.'

'You're nothing but a big fat liar,' said Henry. He was sure Steve was lying. He was absolutely sure Steve was lying. He was one million percent sure that Steve was lying.

He's just trying to pay me back for Christmas, thought Henry.

Steve shrugged. 'Suit yourself. See that stain on the carpet?'

Henry looked down at something brownish.

'That's where the ghost vaporized,' whispered Steve. 'Of course if you're too scared to sleep here . . .'

Henry would rather have walked on hot coals than admit being scared to Steve.

He yawned, as if he'd never heard anything so boring.

'I'm looking forward to meeting the ghost,' said Henry.

'Good,' said Steve.

'Supper, boys!' called Aunt Ruby.

Henry lay in bed. Somehow he'd survived the dreadful meal and Stuck-up Steve's bragging about his expensive clothes, toys and trainers. Now here he was, alone in the attic at the top of the house. He'd jumped into bed, carefully avoiding the faded brown patch on the floor. He was sure it was just spilled cola or something, but just in case . . .

Henry looked around him. The only thing he didn't like was the huge wardrobe opposite the bed. It loomed

up in the darkness at him. You could hide a body in
that wardrobe, thought Henry, then rather wished he
hadn't.

'Ooooooooooh.'

Henry stiffened.

Had he just imagined the sound of someone
moaning?

Silence.

Nothing, thought Henry,
snuggling down under the covers.
Just the wind.

'Ooooooooooh.'

This time the moaning was a fraction louder. The
hairs on Henry's neck stood up. He gripped the sheets
tightly.

'Haaaaaahhhhhhh.'

Henry sat up.

'Haaaaaaaaahhhhhhhhhhhh.'

The ghostly breathy moaning sound was not coming from outside. It appeared to be coming from inside the giant wardrobe.

Quickly, Henry switched on the bedside light.

What am I going to do? thought Henry. He wanted to run screaming to his aunt.

But the truth was, Henry was too frightened to move.

Some dreadful moaning thing was inside the wardrobe.

Just waiting to get *him*.

And then Horrid Henry remembered who he was. Leader of a pirate gang. Afraid of nothing (except injections).

I'll just get up and check inside that wardrobe, he thought. Am I a man or a mouse?

Mouse! he thought.

He did not move.

'Ooooooooaaaaahhhhhh,' moaned the THING. The unearthly noises were getting louder.

Shall I wait here for IT to get me, or shall I make a move first? thought Henry. Silently, he reached under the bed for his Goo-Shooter.

Then slowly, he swung his feet over the bed.

Holding his breath, Horrid Henry stood outside the wardrobe.

'HAHAHAHAHAHAHAHHA!'

Henry jumped. Then he flung open the door and fired.

SPLAT!

'HAHAHAHAHAHAHAHAHAHAHAHA ughhhhhhh –'

The wardrobe was empty.

Except for something small and greeny-black on the top shelf.

It looked like – it was!

Henry reached up and took it.

It was a cassette player. Covered in green goo.

Inside was a tape. It was called 'Dr Jekyll's Spooky Sounds.'

Steve, thought Horrid Henry grimly. REVENGE!

'Did you sleep well, dear?' asked Aunt Ruby at breakfast.

'Like a log,' said Henry.

'No strange noises?' asked Steve.

'No,' smiled Henry sweetly. 'Why, did you hear something?'

Steve looked disappointed. Horrid Henry kept his face blank. He couldn't wait for the evening.

Horrid Henry spent a busy day.
He went ice-skating.
He went to the cinema.
He played football.

After supper, Henry went straight to bed.

'It's been a lovely day,' he said. 'But I'm tired. Goodnight, Aunt Ruby. Goodnight, Steve.'

'Goodnight, Henry,' said Ruby.

Steve ignored him.

But Henry did not go to his bedroom. Instead he sneaked into Steve's.

He wriggled under Steve's bed and lay there, waiting.

Soon Steve came into the room. Henry resisted the urge to reach out and seize Steve's skinny leg. He had something much scarier in mind.

He heard Steve putting on his blue bunny pyjamas and jumping into bed. Henry waited until the room was dark.

Steve lay above him, humming to himself.

'Dooby dooby dooby do,' sang Steve.

Slowly, Henry reached up, and ever so slightly, poked the mattress.

Silence.

'Dooby dooby dooby do,' sang Steve, a little more quietly.

Henry reached up and poked the mattress again.

Steve sat up.

Then he lay back.

Henry poked the mattress again, ever so slightly.

'Must be my imagination,' muttered Steve.

Henry allowed several moments to pass. Then he twitched the duvet.

'Mummy,' whimpered Steve.

Jab! Henry gave the mattress a definite poke.

'AHHHHHHHHHHHH!' screamed Steve. He leaped up and ran out of the room. 'MUMMY! HELP! MONSTERS!'

Henry scrambled out of the room and ran silently up to his attic. Quick as he could he put on his pyjamas, then clattered noisily back down the stairs to Steve's.

Aunt Ruby was on her hands and knees, peering under the bed. Steve was shivering and quivering in the corner.

'There's nothing here, Steve,' she said firmly.

'What's wrong?' asked Henry.

'Nothing,' muttered Steve.

'You're not *scared* of the dark, are you?' said Henry.

'Back to bed, boys,' said Aunt Ruby. She left the room.

'Ahhhhh, Mummy, help! Monsters!' mimicked Henry, sticking out his tongue.

'MUM!' wailed Steve. 'Henry's being horrid!'

'GO TO BED, BOTH OF YOU!' shrieked Ruby.

'Watch out for monsters,' said Henry.

Steve did not move from his corner.

'Want to swap rooms tonight?' said Henry.

Steve did not wait to be asked twice.

'Oh yes,' said Steve.

'Go on up,' said Henry. 'Sweet dreams.'

Steve dashed out of his bedroom as fast as he could.

Tee hee, thought Horrid Henry, pulling Steve's toys down from the shelves. Now, what would he play with first?

Oh, yes. He'd left a few spooky sounds of his own under the attic bed – just in case.

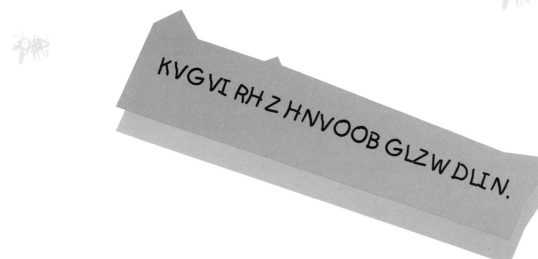

KVGVI RH Z HNVOOB GLZW DLIN.

NRHH YZGGOV-ZCV VZGH MRGH.

BEWARE!! EVIL GROWN-UPS!

Nurse Needle
Most evil crime: giving me an injection

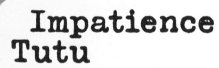

Soggy Sid
Most evil crime: ordering me into the pool

Impatience Tutu
Most evil crime: making me be a raindrop

Ninius Nerdon
Most evil crime: thinking he could beat me

Boudicca Battle-Axe
Most evil crime: being my teacher

Prissy Polly
Most evil crime: forcing me to be a page boy

Pimply Paul
Most evil crime: marrying Prissy Polly

Greasy Greta the Demon Dinner Lady
Most evil crime: nicking my crisps

Fat chance Henny
You're no match for us.
Beware the full moon.
The Secret Club rules

MOODY MARGARET MOVES IN

Mum was on the phone.

'Of course we'd be delighted to have Margaret,' she said. 'It will be no trouble at all.'

Henry stopped breaking the tails off Peter's plastic horses.

'WHAT?' he howled.

'Shh, Henry,' said Mum. 'No, no,' she added. 'Henry is delighted, too. See you Friday.'

'What's going on?' said Henry.

'Margaret is coming to stay while her parents go on holiday,' said Mum.

Henry was speechless with horror.

'She's going to stay . . . here?'

'Yes,' said Mum.

'How long?' said Henry.

'Two weeks,' said Mum brightly.

Horrid Henry could not stand Moody Margaret for more than two minutes.

'Two weeks?' he said. 'I'll run away! I'll lock her out of the house, I'll pull her hair out, I'll . . .'

'Don't be horrid, Henry,' said Mum. 'Margaret's a lovely girl and I'm sure we'll have fun.'

'No we won't,' said Henry. 'Not with that moody old grouch.'

'I'll have fun,' said Perfect Peter. 'I love having guests.'

'She's not sleeping in my room,' said Horrid Henry. 'She can sleep in the cellar.'

'No,' said Mum. 'You'll move into Peter's room and let Margaret have your bed.'

Horrid Henry opened his mouth to scream, but only a rasping sound came out. He was so appalled he could only gasp.

'Give . . . up . . . my . . . room!' he choked. 'To . . . Margaret?'

Margaret spying on *his* treasures, sleeping in *his* bed, playing with *his* toys while he had to share a room with Peter . . .

'No!' howled Henry. He fell on the floor and screamed. 'NO!!'

'I don't mind giving up my bed for a guest,' said Perfect Peter. 'It's the polite thing to do. Guests come first.'

Henry stopped howling just long enough to kick Peter.

'Owww!' screamed Peter. He burst into tears, 'Mum!'

'Henry!' yelled Mum. 'You horrid boy! Say sorry to Peter.'

'She's not coming!' shrieked Henry. 'And that's final.'

'Go to your room!' yelled Mum.

Moody Margaret arrived at Henry's house with her parents, four suitcases, seven boxes of toys, two pillows, and a trumpet.

'Margaret won't be any trouble,' said her mum. 'She's always polite, eats everything, and never complains. Isn't that right, precious?'

'Yes,' said Margaret.

'Margaret's no fusspot,' said her dad. 'She's good as gold, aren't you, precious?'

'Yes,' said Margaret.

'Have a lovely holiday,' said Mum.

'We will,' said Margaret's parents.

The door slammed behind them.

Moody Margaret marched into the sitting room and swept a finger across the mantelpiece.

'It's not very clean, is it?' she said. 'You'd never find so much dust at *my* house.'

'Oh,' said Dad.

'A little dust never hurt anyone,' said Mum.

'I'm allergic,' said Margaret. 'One whiff of dust and I start to . . . sn

. . . sn . . .

ACHOOO!'

she sneezed.

'We'll clean up right away,' said Mum.

Dad mopped.

Mum swept.

Peter dusted.

Henry hoovered.

Margaret directed.

'Henry, you've missed a big dust-ball right there,' said Margaret, pointing under the sofa.

Horrid Henry hoovered as far away from the dust as possible.

'Not there, here!' said Margaret.

Henry aimed the hoover at Margaret. He was a fire-breathing dragon burning his prey to a crisp.

'Help!' shrieked Margaret.

'Henry!' said Dad.

'Don't be horrid,' said Mum.

'I think Henry should be punished,' said Margaret. 'I think he should be locked in his bedroom for three weeks.'

'I don't have a bedroom to be locked up in 'cause you're in it,' said Henry. He glared at Margaret.

Margaret glared back.

'I'm the guest, Henry, so you'd better be polite,' hissed Margaret.

'Of course he'll be polite,' said Mum. 'Don't worry, Margaret. Any trouble, you come straight to me.'

'Thank you,' said Moody Margaret, smiling. 'I will. I'm hungry,' she added. 'Why isn't supper ready?'

'It will be soon,' said Dad.

'But I *always* eat at six o'clock,' said Margaret, 'I want to eat NOW.'

'All right,' said Dad.

Horrid Henry and Moody Margaret dashed for the seat facing the garden. Margaret got there first.

 Henry shoved her off. Then Margaret shoved him off. Thud. Henry landed on the floor. 'Ouch,' said Henry.

'Let the guest have the chair,' said Dad.

'But that's *my* chair,' said Henry. 'That's where I *always* sit.'

'Have my chair, Margaret,' said Perfect Peter. 'I don't mind.'

'I want to sit here,' said Moody Margaret. 'I'm the guest so *I* decide.'

Horrid Henry dragged himself around the table and sat next to Peter.

'OUCH!' shrieked Margaret. 'Henry kicked me!'

'No I didn't,' said Henry, outraged.

'Stop it, Henry,' said Mum. 'That's no way to treat a guest.'

Henry stuck out his tongue at Margaret. Moody Margaret stuck out her tongue even further, then stomped on his foot.

'OUCH!' shrieked Henry. 'Margaret kicked me!'

Moody Margaret gasped. 'Oh I'm ever so sorry, Henry,' she said sweetly. 'It was an accident. Silly me. I didn't mean to, really I didn't.'

Dad brought the food to the table.

'What's *that*?' asked Margaret.

'Baked beans, corn on the cob, and chicken,' said Dad.

'I don't like baked beans,' said Margaret. 'And I like my corn *off* the cob.'

Mum scraped the corn off the cob.

'No, put the corn on a separate plate!' shrieked Margaret. 'I don't like vegetables touching my meat.'

Dad got out the pirate plate, the duck plate, and the 'Happy birthday Peter' plate.

'I want the pirate plate,' said Margaret, snatching it.

'I want the pirate plate,' said Henry, snatching it back.

'I don't mind which plate I get,' said Perfect Peter. 'A plate's a plate.'

'No it isn't!' shouted Henry.

'I'm the guest,' shouted Margaret. 'I get to choose.'

'Give her the pirate plate, Henry,' said Dad.

'It's not fair,' said Henry, glaring at his plate decorated with little ducks.

'She's the guest,' said Mum.

'So?' said Henry. Wasn't there an ancient Greek who stretched all his guests on an iron bed if they were too short or lopped off their heads and feet if they were too long? That guy sure knew how to deal with horrible guests like Moody Margaret.

'Yuck,' said Margaret, spitting out a mouthful of chicken. 'You've put salt on it!'

'Only a little,' said Dad.

'I never eat salt,' said Moody Margaret. 'It's not good for me. And I always have peas at *my* house.'

'We'll get some tomorrow,' said Mum.

Peter lay asleep in the top bunk. Horrid Henry sat listening by the door. He'd scattered crumbs all over Margaret's bed. He couldn't wait to hear her scream.

But there wasn't a sound coming from Henry's room, where Margaret the invader lay. Henry couldn't understand it.

Sadly, he climbed into (oh, the shame of it) the *bottom* bunk. Then he screamed. His bed was filled with jam, crumbs, and something squishy squashy and horrible.

'Go to sleep, Henry!' shouted Dad.

That Margaret! He'd booby-trap the room, cut up her doll's clothes, paint her face purple . . . Henry smiled grimly. Oh yes, he'd fix Moody Margaret.

Mum and Dad sat in the sitting room watching TV.

Moody Margaret appeared on the stairs.

'I can't sleep with that noise,' she said.

Mum and Dad looked at each other.

'We are watching very quietly, dear,' said Mum.

'But I can't sleep if there's any noise in the house,' said Margaret. 'I have very sensitive ears.'

Mum turned off the TV and picked up her knitting needles.

Click click click.

Margaret reappeared.

'I can't sleep with that clicking noise,' she said.

'All right,' said Mum. She sighed a little.

'And it's cold in my bedroom,' said Moody Margaret.

Mum turned up the heat.

Margaret reappeared.

'Now it's too hot,' said Moody Margaret.

Dad turned down the heat.

'My room smells funny,' said Margaret.

'My bed is too hard,' said Margaret.

'My room is too stuffy,' said Margaret.

'My room is too light,' said Margaret.

'Goodnight, Margaret,' said Mum.

'How many more days is she staying?' said Dad.

Mum looked at the calendar.

'Only thirteen,' said Mum.

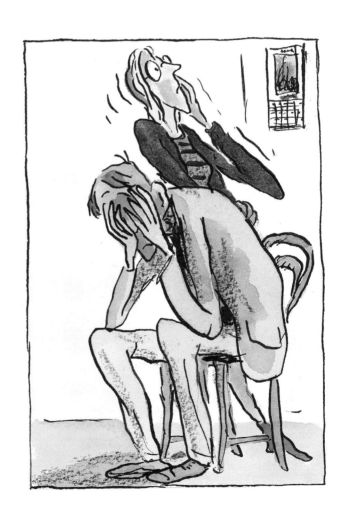

Dad hid his face in his hands.

'I don't know if I can live that long,' said Dad.

$$\sim\!\!\sim\!\!\sim\!\!\sim$$

TOOT A TOOT.
Mum blasted out of bed.
TOOT A TOOT. Dad blasted out of bed.
**TOOT A TOOT. TOOT A TOOT. TOOT A
TOOT TOOT TOOT.** Henry and Peter blasted out
of bed.

Margaret marched down the hall, playing her
trumpet.
**TOOT A TOOT. TOOT A TOOT. TOOT A
TOOT TOOT TOOT TOOT.**

'Margaret, would you mind playing your trumpet a
little later?' said Dad, clutching his ears. 'It's six o'clock
in the morning.'

'That's when I wake up,' said Margaret.

'Could you play a little more softly?' said Mum.

'But I have to practise,' said Moody Margaret.

The trumpet blared through the house.
TOOT TOOT TOOT.
Horrid Henry turned on his boom box.
BOOM BOOM BOOM.

88

Margaret played her trumpet louder.

TOOT! TOOT! TOOT!

Henry blasted his boom box as loud as he could.

BOOM! BOOM! BOOM!

'Henry!' shrieked Mum.

'Turn that down!' bellowed Dad.

'Quiet!' screamed Margaret. 'I can't practise with all this noise.' She put down her trumpet. 'And I'm hungry. Where's my breakfast?'

'We have breakfast at eight,' said Mum.

'But I want breakfast now,' said Margaret.

Mum had had enough.

'No,' said Mum firmly. 'We eat at eight.'

Margaret opened her mouth and screamed. No one could scream as long, or as loud, as Moody Margaret.

Her piercing screams echoed through the house.

'All right,' said Mum. She knew when she was beaten. 'We'll eat now.'

Henry's diary

Monday I put crumbs in Margaret's bed. She put jam, crusts and slugs in mine.

Tuesday Margaret found my secret biscuits and crisps and ate every single one.

Wednesday I can't play tapes at night because it disturbs grumpy-face Margaret.

Thursday I can't sing because it disturbs frog-face.

Friday I can't breathe because it disturbs misery-guts.

Saturday I can stand it No Longer

That night, when everyone was asleep, Horrid Henry crept into the sitting room and picked up the phone.

'I'd like to leave a message,' he whispered.

Bang bang bang bang bang.

Ding dong! Ding dong! Ding dong!

Henry sat up in bed.

Someone was banging on the front door and ringing the bell.

'Who could that be at this time of night?' yawned Mum.

Dad peeked through the window then opened the door.

'Where's my baby?' shouted Margaret's mum.

'Where's my baby?' shouted Margaret's dad.

'Upstairs,' said Mum. 'Where else?'

'What's happened to her?' shrieked Margaret's mum.

'We got here as quick as we could!' shrieked Margaret's dad.

Mum and Dad looked at each other. What was going on?

'She's fine,' said Mum.

Margaret's mum and dad looked at each other. What was going on?

'But the message said it was an emergency and to come at once,' said Margaret's mum.

'We cut short our holiday,' said Margaret's dad.

'What message?' said Mum.

'What's going on? I can't sleep with all this noise,' said Moody Margaret.

Margaret and her parents had gone home.

'What a terrible mix-up,' said Mum.

'Such a shame they cut short their holiday,' said Dad.

'Still . . .' said Mum. She looked at Dad.

'Hmmn,' said Dad.

'You don't think that Henry . . .' said Mum.

'Not even Henry could do something so horrid,' said Dad.

Mum frowned.

'Henry!' said Mum.

Henry continued sticking Peter's stamps together. 'Yeah?'

'Do you know anything about a message?'

'Me?' said Henry.

'You,' said Mum.

'No,' said Henry. 'It's a mystery.'

'That's a lie, Henry,' said Perfect Peter.

'Is not,' said Henry.

'Is too,' said Peter. 'I heard you on the phone.'

Henry lunged at Peter. He was a mad bull charging the matador.

'YOWWWWW,' shrieked Peter.

Henry stopped. He was in for it now. No pocket money for a year. No sweets for ten years. No TV ever.

Henry squared his shoulders and waited for his punishment.

Dad put his feet up.

'That was a terrible thing to do,' said Dad.

Mum turned on the TV.

'Go to your room,' said Mum.

Henry bounced upstairs. Your room. Sweeter words were never spoken.

Dear Henry, Peter and Parents,

I think you should know all the things that are wrong at your house so that you can do better next time.

1. Everyone should go to bed when I do at 8.30 pm and not make any noise.
2. Guests should always be given the pirate plate.
3. Guests should always decide where they sit at the table.
4. I am allergic to dust. Clean your house more or I won't come back.
5. My breakfast should be served when I wake up at 6.30 am and not one minute later.
6. If you break my egg yolk you must start again.
7. You cooked lots of things I don't like. You should have asked me first. No baked beans. No corn on the cob. No salt.
8. Henry must be locked in his room with bread and water while I am staying.
9. If I think of anything else I will tell you.

Margaret

P.S. Thank you for having me to stay.

WANTED

DEAD OR ALIVE

Worlds most horrible girl

Guilty of
attacking Henry's Purple Hand Fort
putting jam crusts and slugs in
  Henry's bed;
annoying him, and other crimes

EVIL ENEMY

Moody Margaret

NZITZI VG RH Z KLGZGL.

HORRID HENRY'S RAID

'**Y**ou're such a pig, Susan!'

'No I'm not! You're the pig!'

'You are!' squealed Moody Margaret.

'You are!' squealed Sour Susan.

'Oink!'

'Oink!'

All was not well at Moody Margaret's Secret Club.

Sour Susan and Moody Margaret glared at each other inside the Secret Club tent. Moody Margaret waved the empty biscuit tin in Susan's sour face.

'*Someone* ate all the biscuits,' said Moody Margaret. 'And it wasn't me.'

'Well, it wasn't me,' said Susan.

'Liar!'

'Liar!'

Margaret stuck out her tongue at Susan.

Susan stuck out her tongue at Margaret.

Margaret yanked Susan's hair.

'Oww! You horrible meanie!' shrieked Susan. 'I hate you.'

She yanked Margaret's hair.

'OWWW!' screeched Moody Margaret. 'How dare you?'

They scowled at each other.

'Wait a minute,' said Margaret. 'You don't think –'

Not a million miles away, sitting on a throne inside the Purple Hand fort hidden behind prickly branches, Horrid Henry wiped a few biscuit crumbs from his mouth and burped. Umm, boy, nothing beat the taste of an arch-enemy's biscuits.

The branches parted.

'Password!' hissed Horrid Henry.

'Smelly toads.'

'Enter,' said Henry.

The sentry entered and gave the secret handshake.

'Henry, why –' began Perfect Peter.

'Call me by my title, Worm!'

'Sorry, Henry – I mean Lord High Excellent Majesty of the Purple Hand.'

'That's better,' said Henry. He waved his hand and

pointed at the ground. 'Be seated, Worm.'

'Why am I Worm and you're Lord High Excellent Majesty?'

'Because I'm the Leader,' said Henry.

'I want a better title,' said Peter.

'All right,' said the Lord High Excellent Majesty, 'you can be Lord Worm.'

Peter considered.

'What about Lord High Worm?'

'OK,' said Henry. Then he froze.

'Worm! Footsteps!'

Perfect Peter peeked through the leaves.

'Enemies approaching!' he warned.

Pounding feet paused outside the entrance.

'Password!' said Horrid Henry.

'Dog poo breath,' said Margaret, bursting in. Sour Susan followed.

'That's not the password,' said Henry.

'You can't come in,' squeaked the sentry, a little late.

'You've been stealing the Secret Club biscuits,' said Moody Margaret.

'Yeah, Henry,' said Susan.

Horrid Henry stretched and yawned.

'Prove it.'

Moody Margaret pointed to all the crumbs lying on the dirt floor.

'Where did all these crumbs come from, then?'

'Biscuits,' said Henry.

'So you admit it!' shrieked Margaret.

'Purple Hand biscuits,' said Henry. He pointed to the Purple Hand skull and crossbones biscuit tin.

'Liar, liar, pants on fire,' said Margaret.

Horrid Henry fell to the floor and started rolling around.

'Ooh, ooh, my pants are on fire, I'm burning, call the fire brigade!' shouted Henry.

Perfect Peter dashed off. 'Mum!' he hollered. 'Henry's pants are on fire!'

Margaret and Susan made a hasty retreat.

Horrid Henry stopped rolling and howled with laughter.

'Ha ha ha ha ha – the Purple Hand rules!' he cackled.

'We'll get you for this, Henry,' said Margaret.

'Yeah, yeah,' said Henry.

'You didn't really steal their biscuits, did you Henry?' asked Lord High Worm the following day.

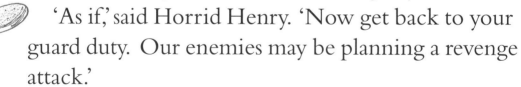

'As if,' said Horrid Henry. 'Now get back to your guard duty. Our enemies may be planning a revenge attack.'

'Why do I always have to be the guard?' said Peter. 'It's not fair.'

'Whose club is this?' said Henry fiercely.

Peter's lip began to tremble.

'Yours,' muttered Peter.

'So if you want to stay as a temporary

member, you have to do what I say,' said Henry.

'OK,' said Peter.

'And remember, one day, if you're very good, you'll be promoted from junior sentry to chief sentry,' said Henry.

'Ooh,' said Peter, brightening.

Business settled, Horrid Henry reached for the biscuit tin. He'd saved five yummy chocolate fudge chewies for today.

Henry picked up the tin and stopped. Why wasn't it rattling? He shook it.

Silence.

Horrid Henry ripped off the lid and shrieked.

The Purple Hand biscuit tin was empty. Except for one thing. A dagger drawn on a piece of paper. The dastardly mark of Margaret's Secret Club! Well, he'd show them who ruled.

'Worm!' he shrieked. 'Get in here!'

Peter entered.

'We've been raided!' screamed Henry. 'You're fired!'

'Waaaah!' wailed Peter.

'Good work, Susan,' said the Leader of the Secret Club, her face covered in chocolate.

'I don't see why you got three biscuits and I only got two when I was the one who sneaked in and stole them,' said Susan sourly.

'Tribute to your Leader,' said Moody Margaret.

'I still don't think it's fair,' muttered Susan.

'Tough,' said Margaret. 'Now let's hear your spy report.'

'NAH NAH NEE NAH NAH!' screeched a voice from outside.

Susan and Margaret dashed out of the Secret Club tent. They were too late. There was Henry, prancing off, waving the Secret Club banner he'd stolen.

'Give that back, Henry!' screamed Margaret.

'Make me!' said Henry.

Susan chased him. Henry darted.
Margaret chased him. Henry dodged.
'Come and get me!' taunted Henry.

'All right,' said Margaret. She walked towards him,
then suddenly jumped over the wall into Henry's
garden and ran to the Purple Hand fort.

'Hey, get away from there!' shouted Henry, chasing
after her. Where was that useless sentry when you
needed him?

Margaret nabbed Henry's skull and crossbones flag,
and darted off.

The two Leaders faced each other.

'Gimme my flag!' ordered Henry.

'Gimme my flag!' ordered Margaret.

'You first,' said Henry.

'*You* first,' said Margaret.

Neither moved.

'OK, at the count of three we'll throw them to each
other,' said Margaret. 'One, two, three – throw!'

Margaret held on to Henry's flag.
Henry held on to Margaret's flag.
Several moments passed.
'Cheater,' said Margaret.
'Cheater,' said Henry.

Down with girls

'I don't know about you, but I have important spying work to get on with,' said Margaret.

'So?' said Henry. 'Get on with it. No one's stopping you.'

'Drop my flag, Henry,' said Margaret.

'No,' said Henry.

'Fine,' said Margaret. 'Susan! Bring me the scissors.'

Susan ran off.

'Peter!' shouted Henry. 'Worm! Lord Worm! Lord High Worm!'

Peter stuck his head out of the upstairs window.

'Peter! Fetch the scissors! Quick!' ordered Henry.

'No,' said Peter. 'You fired me, remember?' And he slammed the window shut.

'You're dead, Peter,' shouted Henry.

Sour Susan came back with the scissors and gave them to Margaret. Margaret held the scissors to Henry's flag. Henry didn't budge. She wouldn't dare –

Snip!

Aaargh! Moody Margaret cut off a corner of Henry's flag. She held the scissors poised to make another cut.

Horrid Henry had spent hours painting his beautiful flag. He knew when he was beaten.

'Stop!' shrieked Henry.

He dropped Margaret's flag. Margaret dropped his

flag. Slowly, they inched towards each other, then dashed to grab their own flag.

'Truce?' said Moody Margaret, beaming.

'Truce,' said Horrid Henry, scowling.

I'll get her for this, thought Horrid Henry. No one touches my flag and lives.

Horrid Henry watched and waited until it was dark and he heard the plinky-plonk sound of Moody Margaret practising her piano.

The coast was

clear. Horrid Henry sneaked outside, jumped over the wall and darted inside the Secret Club Tent.

Swoop! He swept up the Secret Club pencils and secret code book.

Snatch! He snaffled the Secret Club stool.

Grab! He bagged the Secret Club biscuit tin.

Was that everything?

No!

Scoop! He snatched the Secret Club motto ('Down with boys').

Pounce! He pinched the Secret Club carpet.

Horrid Henry looked around. The Secret Club tent was bare.

Except for –

Henry considered. Should he?

Yes!

Whisk! The Secret Club tent collapsed. Henry gathered it into his arms with the rest of his spoils.

Huffing and puffing, gasping and panting, Horrid Henry staggered off over the wall, laden with the Secret Club. Raiding was hot, heavy work, but a pirate had to do his duty. Wouldn't all this booty look great decorating his fort? A rug on the floor, an extra biscuit tin, a repainted motto – 'Down with girls' – yes, the Purple Hand Fort would have to be renamed the Purple Hand Palace.

Speaking of which, where was the Purple Hand Fort?

Horrid Henry looked about wildly for the Fort entrance.

It was gone.

He searched for the Purple Hand throne.

It was gone.

And the Purple Hand biscuit tin – GONE!

There was a rustling sound in the shadows. Horrid Henry turned and saw a strange sight.

There was the Purple Hand Fort leaning against the shed.

What?!

Suddenly the Fort started moving. Slowly, jerkily, the Fort wobbled across the lawn towards the wall on its four new stumpy legs.

Horrid Henry was livid. How dare someone try to nick his fort! This was an outrage. What was the world coming to, when people just sneaked into your garden and made off with your fort? Well, no way!

Horrid Henry let out a pirate roar.

'RAAAAAAAA!' roared Horrid Henry.

'AHHHHHHH!' shrieked the Fort.

CRASH!

The Purple Hand Fort fell to the ground. The raiders ran off, squabbling.

'I told you to hurry, you lazy lump!'

'You're the lazy lump!'

Victory!

Horrid Henry climbed to the top of his fort and grabbed his banner. Waving it proudly, he chanted his victory chant:

NAH NAH NE NAH NAH!

Catapult them
into a moat filled
with piranha fish

Let crocodiles
loose in their
bedrooms

Exile to an island
with no TV

Make them eat
chool dinners

How to Get
Rid of
EVIL
ENEMIES

Dump them in
snakepits

Drop them in
vats of glop

BEWARE!!
EVIL GROWN-UPS!

Nurse Needle

Rabid Rebecca

Miss Battle-Axe

Greasy Greta,
the Demon Dinner
lady

HORRID HENRY GOES TO WORK

'It's your turn!'

'No, it's yours!'

'Yours!'

'Yours!'

'I took Henry last year!' said Mum.

Dad paused. 'Are you sure?'

'YES,' said Mum.

'Are you sure you're sure?' said Dad. He looked pale.

'Of course I'm sure!' said Mum. 'How could I forget?'

Tomorrow was take your child to work day. Mum wanted to take Peter. Dad wanted to take Peter. Unfortunately, someone had to take Henry.

Only today Dad's boss had said how much he was looking forward to meeting Dad's lovely son. 'Of course I'll be bringing my boy, Bill,' said Big Boss. 'He's a great kid. Good as gold. Smart as a whip. Superb footballer. Brilliant at maths. Plays trumpet like a genius. Perfect manners. Yep, I sure am proud of Bill.'

Dad tried not to hate Bill. He failed.

'Now listen, Henry,' said Dad. 'You're coming to work with me tomorrow. I'm warning you, my boss is bringing *his* son. From what I hear he's perfect.'

'Like me?' said Peter. 'I'd love to meet him. We

could swap good deed ideas! Do you think he'd like to join my Best Boys Club?'

'You're going to Mum's work,' said Dad sadly. 'I'm taking Henry.'

'Cool!' said Henry. A day out of school! A day at the office! 'I want to play computer games. And eat doughnuts! And surf the web!'

'NO!' said Dad. 'An office is a place where people work. I want perfect behaviour. My boss is very strict. Don't let me down, Henry.'

'Of course I won't,' said Horrid Henry. He was outraged. How could Dad think such a thing? The only trouble was, how could Henry have any fun with a boring goody-goody like Bill around?

'Remember what I said, Henry,' said Dad the next morning, as they arrived at his office. 'Be nice to Bill. Do what he says. He's the boss's son. Try to be as good as he is.'

'All right,' said Henry sourly.

Dad's boss came to welcome them.

'Ah, you must be Henry!' said Big Boss. 'This is my son, Bill.'

'So pleased to meet you, Henry,' said Bossy Bill.

'Huh,' grunted Horrid Henry.

He looked at Bossy Bill. He was wearing a jacket and tie. His face was gleaming. His shoes were so polished Henry could see his dirty face in them. Just his luck to get stuck all day with boring old Bossy Bill.

'Right, boys, your first job is to make tea for everyone in the meeting room,' said Big Boss.

'Do I have to?' said Horrid Henry.

'Henry!' said Dad.

'Yes,' said Big Boss. 'That's six teas, one sugar in each.'

'Gee thanks, Dad!' said Bossy Bill. 'I love making tea.'

'Whoopee,' muttered Horrid Henry.

Big Boss beamed and left the room. Horrid Henry was alone with Bossy Bill.

The moment Big Boss left, Bill's face changed.

'Why doesn't he make his own stupid tea!' he snarled.

'I thought you loved making tea,' said Horrid Henry. Maybe things were looking up.

'No way,' said Bossy Bill. 'What am I, a servant? You make it.'

'You make it!' said Horrid Henry.

'You make it!' said Bossy Bill.

'No,' said Henry.

'Yes,' said Bill. 'It's my dad's company and you have to do what I say.'

'No I don't!' said Henry.

'Yes you do,' said Bill.

'I don't work for you,' said Henry.

'Yeah, but your dad works for *my* dad,' said Bossy Bill. 'If you don't do what I say I'll tell my dad to fire your dad.'

Horrid Henry glared at Bossy Bill, then slowly switched on the kettle. When he was king he'd build a shark tank specially for Bill.

Bossy Bill folded his arms and smirked as Henry poured hot water over the teabags. What a creep, thought Henry, licking his fingers and dipping them into the sugar bowl.

'You're disgusting,' said Bossy Bill. 'I'm telling on you.'

'Go ahead,' said Henry, licking sugar off his fingers. Next to his cousin Stuck-up Steve, Bossy Bill was the yuckiest kid he had ever met.

'Hey, I've got a great idea,' said Bill. 'Let's put salt in the tea instead of sugar.'

Horrid Henry hesitated. But hadn't Dad said to do what Bill told him?

'OK,' said Henry.

Bossy Bill poured a heaped teaspoon of salt into every cup.

'Now watch this,' said Bill.

'Thank you, Bill,' said Mr String. 'Aren't you clever!'

'Thank you, Bill,' said Ms Bean. 'Aren't you wonderful!'

'Thanks, Bill,' said Big Boss. 'How's the tea, everyone?'

'Delicious,' said Mr String. He put down the cup.

'Delightful,' said Ms Bean. She put down the cup.

'Umm,' said Dad. He put down the cup.

Then Big Boss took a sip. His face curdled.

'Disgusting!' he gasped, spitting out the tea. 'Bleeecch! Who put salt in this?'

'Henry did,' said Bill.

Horrid Henry was outraged.

'Liar!' said Henry. 'You did!'

'This tea is revolting,' said Mr String.

'Horrible,' said Ms Bean.

'I tried to stop him, Dad, but he just wouldn't

listen,' said Bossy Bill.

'I'm disappointed in you, Henry,' said Big Boss. 'Bill would never do anything like this.' He glanced at Dad. Dad looked as if he wished an alien spaceship would beam him up.

'But I didn't do it!' said Henry. He stared at Bill. What a creep!

'Now run along boys, and help answer the phones. Bill will show you how, Henry,' said Big Boss.

Horrid Henry followed Bill out of the meeting room. Beware, Bill, he thought. I'll get you for this.

Bill sat down at a huge desk and swung his feet up.

'Now copy me,' he said. 'Answer the phones just like I do.'

Ring ring.

'Hello, Elephant House!' said Bill.

Ring ring.

'Hello! Tootsie's Take-Away!' said Bill.

Ring ring.

'Hello! Pizza Parlour!' said Bill.

Ring ring.

'Go on, Henry, answer it.'

'No!' said Henry. After what had just happened with the tea, he'd never trust Bill again.

Ring ring.

'What are you, chicken?' said Bill.

'No,' said Henry.

'Then go on. *I* did it.'

Ring ring ring ring.

'All right,' said Henry. He picked up the phone. He'd just do it once.

'Hello Smelly! You're fired!'

Silence.

'Is that you, Henry?' said

Big Boss on the other end of the phone.

Eeek!

'Wrong number!' squeaked
Horrid Henry, and slammed down
the phone. Uh oh. Now he was in trouble. Big big
trouble.

Big Boss stormed into the room.

'What's going on in here?'

'I tried to stop him, but he just wouldn't listen,' said
Bossy Bill.

'That's not true!' squealed Horrid Henry. 'You
started it.'

'As if,' said Bossy Bill.

'And what have you been doing, son?' asked Big
Boss.

'Testing the phones for you,' said Bossy Bill. 'I think
there's a fault on line 2. I'll fix it in a minute.'

'That's my little genius,' beamed Big Boss.
He glared at Henry. Henry glared back.

'I told you to follow Bill's example!'
hissed Dad.

'I did!' hissed Henry.

Bossy Bill and Big Boss exchanged pitying glances.

'He's not usually like this,' lied Dad. He looked as if
he wished a whirlwind would whisk him away.

'I am usually like this!' said Henry. 'Just not today!'

'No pocket money for a year if there's any more

trouble,' muttered Dad.

This was so unfair. Why should he get blamed when it was absolutely definitely not his fault?

'I'll give you one more chance,' said Big Boss. He handed Henry a stack of papers. 'Photocopy these for the meeting this afternoon,' he said. 'If there are any more problems I will ask your father to take you home.'

Take him home! Dad would never ever forgive him. He was mad enough at Henry already. And it was all Bill's fault.

Scowling, Horrid Henry followed Bill into the photocopy room.

'Ha ha ha ha ha, I got you into trouble!' chortled Bill.

Horrid Henry resisted the urge to mash Bossy Bill into tiny bite-sized chunks. Instead, Horrid Henry started to think. Even if he was good as gold all day it would mean Bill had won. He had to come up with a plan to get back at Bill. Fast. But what? Anything awful Bill did Henry was sure to get the blame. No one would believe Henry hadn't done it. If his plan was to work, Bill had to be caught red-handed.

And then Horrid Henry had it. A perfectly brilliant, spectacularly evil plan. A plan to end all plans. A plan to go down in history. A plan – but there was no time to lose congratulating himself.

Bossy Bill snatched the papers from Henry's hand.

'I get to do the photocopying because it's *my* dad's office,' he said. 'If you're good I might let you hand out the papers.'

'Whatever you say,' said Horrid Henry humbly. 'After all, you're the boss.'

'Too right I am,' said Bossy Bill. 'Everyone has to do what I say.'

'Of course,' said Horrid Henry agreeably. 'Hey, I've got a great idea,' he added after a moment, 'why don't we make horrid faces, photocopy them and hang the pictures all round the meeting room?'

Bossy Bill's eyes gleamed.

'Yeah!' he said. He stuck out his tongue. He made a monkey face. He twisted his lips. 'Heh heh heh.' Then he paused. 'Wait a minute. We'd be recognised.'

Aaargh! Horrid Henry hadn't thought of that. His beautiful plan crumpled before him. Bill would win. Henry would lose. The terrible image of Bossy Bill laughing at him from here to eternity loomed before him. NO! No one ever tricked Horrid Henry and lived. I need a change of plan, thought Henry desperately. And then he knew what had to be done. It was risky. It was dangerous. But it was the only way.

'I know,' said Horrid Henry. 'Let's photocopy our bottoms instead.'

'Yeah!' said Bossy Bill. 'I was just going to suggest that.'

'I get to go first,' said Horrid Henry, shoving Bill out of the way.

'No, I do!' said Bill, shoving him back.

YES! thought Horrid Henry, as Bill hopped onto the photocopier. '*You* can paste up the pictures in the meeting room.'

'Great!' said Henry. He could tell what Bill was thinking. He'd get his dad to come in while Henry was sellotaping pictures of bottoms around the meeting room.

'I'll just get the sellotape,' said Henry.

'You do that,' said Bossy Bill, as the photocopier whirred into life.

Horrid Henry ran down the hall into Big Boss's office.

'Come quick, Bill's in trouble!' said Horrid Henry.

Big Boss dropped the phone and raced down the hall after Henry.

'Hold on, Bill, Daddy's coming!' he shrieked, and burst into the photocopy room.

There was Bossy Bill, perched on the photocopier, his back to the door, singing merrily:

'One bottom,
two bottoms,
three bottoms,
four,
Five bottoms,
six bottoms,
seven bottoms,
more!'

'Bill!' screamed Big Boss.

'It was Henry!' screamed Bossy Bill. 'I was just testing the photocopier to make sure –'

'Be quiet, Bill!' shouted Big Boss. 'I saw what you were doing.'

'I tried to stop him but he just wouldn't listen,' said Horrid Henry.

Horrid Henry spent a lovely rest of the day at Dad's office. After Bill was grounded for a month and sent home in disgrace, Henry twirled all the chairs round and round. He sneaked up behind people and shouted, 'Boo!' Then he ate doughnuts, played computer games, and surfed the web. Boy, working in an office is fun, thought Horrid Henry. I'm going to enjoy getting a job when I grow up.

EVIL ENEMY

Bossy Bill

YROO SZH Z YRT SFT V TRMLI NLFH YLGGLN.

BATTLE PLANS

Sneak into Secret Club tent and **raid** biscuit tin while Margaret is practising her trumpet.

Spy on Secret Club meetings and foil all their evil plans.

Stinkbombs!

Boobytrap their club with a bucket of water over the entrance.

HORRID HENRY'S STINK BOMB

'I hate you, Margaret!' shrieked Sour Susan. She stumbled out of the Secret Club tent.

'I hate you too!' shrieked Moody Margaret.

Sour Susan stuck out her tongue.

Moody Margaret stuck out hers back.

'I quit!' yelled Susan.

'You can't quit. You're fired!' yelled Margaret.

'You can't fire me. I quit!' said Susan.

'I fired you first,' said Margaret. 'And I'm changing the password!'

'Go ahead. See if I care. I don't want to be in the Secret Club any more!' said Susan sourly.

'Good! Because *we* don't want you.'

Moody Margaret flounced back inside the Secret Club tent. Sour Susan stalked off.

Free at last! Susan was sick and tired of her ex-best friend Bossyboots Margaret. Blaming *her* for the disastrous raid on the Purple Hand Fort when it was all Margaret's fault was bad enough. But then to ask stupid Linda to join the Secret Club without even telling her! Susan hated Linda even more than she hated Margaret. Linda hadn't invited

Ha ha Margaret,
You stink and so does
your pongy old club.
The Purple Hand

Susan to her sleepover party. And she was a copycat. But Margaret didn't care. Today she'd made Linda chief spy. Well, Susan had had enough. Margaret had been mean to her once too often.

Susan heard gales of laughter from inside the club tent. So they were laughing, were they? Laughing at her, no doubt? Well, she'd show them. She knew all about Margaret's Top Secret Plans. And she knew someone who would be very interested in that information.

'Halt! Password!'

'Smelly toads,' said Perfect Peter. He waited outside Henry's Purple Hand Fort.

'Wrong,' said Horrid Henry.

'What's the new one then?' said Perfect Peter.

'I'm not telling *you*,' said Henry. 'You're fired, remember?'

Perfect Peter did remember. He had hoped Henry had forgotten.

'Can't I join again, Henry?' asked Peter.

'No way!' said Horrid Henry.

'Please?' said Perfect Peter.

'No,' said Horrid Henry. 'Ralph's taken over your duties.'

Rude Ralph poked his head through the branches of Henry's lair.

'No babies allowed,' said Rude Ralph.

'We don't want you here, Peter,' said Horrid Henry. 'Get lost.'

Perfect Peter burst into tears.

'Crybaby!' jeered Horrid Henry.

'Crybaby!' jeered Rude Ralph.

That did it.

'Mum!' wailed Perfect Peter. He ran towards the house. 'Henry won't let me play and he called me a crybaby!'

'Stop being horrid, Henry!' shouted Mum.

Peter waited.

Mum didn't say anything else.

Perfect Peter started to wail louder.

'Muuum! Henry's being mean to me!'

'Leave Peter alone, Henry!' shouted Mum. She came out of the house. Her hands were covered in dough. 'Henry, if you don't stop –'

Mum looked around.

'Where's Henry?'

'In his fort,' snivelled Peter.

'I thought you said he was being mean to you,' said Mum.

'He was!' wailed Peter.

'Just keep away from him,' said Mum. She went back into the house.

Perfect Peter was outraged. Was that it? Why hadn't she punished Henry? Henry had been so horrid he deserved to go to prison for a year. Two years. And just get a crust of bread a week. And brussels sprouts. Ha! That would serve Henry right.

But until Henry went to prison, how could Peter pay him back?

And then Peter knew exactly what he could do.

He checked carefully to see that no one was watching. Then he sneaked over the garden wall and headed for the Secret Club Tent.

'He isn't!' said Margaret.

'She wouldn't,' said Henry.

'He's planning to swap our lemonade for a Dungeon Drink?' said Margaret.

'Yes,' said Peter.

She's planning to stinkbomb the Purple Hand Fort?' said Henry.

'Yes,' said Susan.

'How dare she?' said Henry.

'How dare he?' said Margaret. 'I'll easily put a stop to that. Linda!' she barked. 'Hide the lemonade!'

Linda yawned.

'Hide it yourself,' she said. 'I'm tired.'

Margaret glared at her, then hid the jug under a box.

'Ha ha! Won't Henry be shocked when he sneaks over and there are no drinks to spike!' gloated Margaret. 'Peter, you're a hero. I award you the Triple Star, the highest honour the Secret Club can bestow.'

'Ooh, thanks!' said Peter. It was nice being appreciated for a change.

'So from now on,' said Moody Margaret, 'you're working for me.'

'Okay,' said the traitor.

Horrid Henry rubbed his hands. This was fantastic! At last, he had a spy in the enemy's camp! He'd easily defend himself against that stupid stinkbomb. Margaret would only let it off when he was *in* the fort. His sentry would be on the lookout armed with a goo-shooter. When Margaret tried to sneak in with her stinkbomb — ker-pow!

'Hang on a sec,' said Horrid Henry, 'why should I trust you?'

'Because Margaret is mean and horrible and I hate her,' said Susan.

'So from now on,' said Horrid Henry, 'you're working for me.'

Susan wasn't sure she liked the sound of that. Then she remembered Margaret's mean cackle.

'Okay,' said the traitor.

Peter sneaked back into his garden and collided with someone.

'Ouch!' said Peter.

'Watch where you're going!' snapped Susan.

They glared at each other suspiciously.

'What were you doing at Margaret's?' said Susan.

'Nothing,' said Peter. 'What were you doing at my house?'

'Nothing,' said Susan.

Peter walked towards Henry's fort, whistling.

Susan walked towards Margaret's tent, whistling.

Well, if Susan was spying on Henry for Margaret, Peter certainly wasn't going to warn him. Serve Henry right.

Well, if Peter was spying on Margaret for Henry,

Susan certainly wasn't going to warn her. Serve Margaret right.

Dungeon Drinks, eh?

Margaret liked that idea much better than her stinkbomb plot.

'I've changed my mind about the stinkbomb,' said Margaret. 'I'm going to swap his drinks for Dungeon Drink stinkers instead.'

'Good idea,' said Lazy Linda. 'Less work.'

Stinkbomb, eh?

Henry liked that much better than his dungeon drink plot. Why hadn't he thought of that himself?

'I've changed my mind about the Dungeon Drinks,' said Henry. 'I'm going to stinkbomb her instead.'

'Yeah,' said Rude Ralph. 'When?'

'Now,' said Horrid Henry. 'Come on, let's go to my room.'

Horrid Henry opened his Stinky Stinkbomb kit. He'd bought it with Grandma. Mum would *never* have let him buy it. But because Grandma had given him the money Mum couldn't do anything about it. Ha ha ha.

Now, which pong would he pick? He looked at the test tubes filled with powder and read the gruesome labels.

Bad breath. Dog poo. Rotten eggs. Smelly socks. Dead fish. Sewer stench.

'I'd go for dead fish,' said Ralph. 'That's the worst.' Henry considered.

'How about we mix dead fish *and* rotten eggs?'

'Yeah,' said Rude Ralph.

Slowly, carefully, Horrid Henry measured out a teaspoon of Dead Fish powder, and a teaspoon of Rotten Egg powder, into the special pouch.

Slowly, carefully, Rude Ralph poured out 150 millilitres of secret stinkbomb liquid into the bottle and capped it tightly.

All they had to do was to add the powder to the bottle outside the Secret Club and— run!

'Ready?' said Horrid Henry.

'Ready,' said Rude Ralph.

'Whatever you do,' said Horrid Henry, 'don't spill it.'

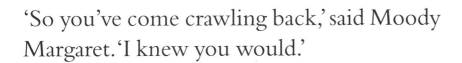

'So you've come crawling back,' said Moody Margaret. 'I knew you would.'

'No,' said Sour Susan. 'I just happened to be passing.'

She looked around the Secret Club Tent.

'Where's Linda?'

Margaret scowled. 'Gone.'

'Gone for today, or gone for ever?' said Susan.

'For ever,' said Margaret savagely. 'I don't ever want to see that lazy lump again.'

Margaret and Susan looked at each other.

Susan tapped her foot.

Margaret hummed.

'Well?' said Margaret.

'Well what?' said Susan.

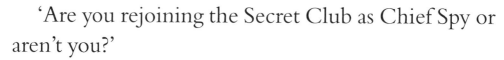

'Are you rejoining the Secret Club as Chief Spy or aren't you?'

'I might,' said Susan. 'And I might not.'

'Suit yourself,' said Margaret. 'I'll call Gurinder and ask her to join instead.'

'Okay,' said Susan quickly. 'I'll join.'

Should she mention her visit to Henry? Better not. After all, what Margaret didn't know wouldn't hurt her.

'Now, about my stinkbomb plot,' began Margaret. 'I decided –'

Something shattered on the ground inside the tent. A ghastly, gruesome, grisly stinky stench filled the air.

'AAAAARGGGGG!' screamed Margaret, gagging.

'It's a — STINKBOMB!'

'HELP!' shrieked Sour Susan. 'STINKBOMB! Help! Help!'

Victory! Horrid Henry and Rude Ralph ran back to the Purple Hand Fort and rolled round the floor, laughing and shrieking.

What a triumph! Margaret and Susan screaming! Margaret's mum screaming! Margaret's dad screaming! And the stink! Wow! Horrid Henry had never smelled anything so awful in his life.

This called for a celebration.

Horrid Henry offered Ralph a fistful of sweets and poured out two glasses of Fizzywizz drinks.

'Cheers!' said Henry.

'Cheers!' said Ralph.

They drank.

'AAAAAARRGGGGGG!' choked Rude Ralph.

'Bleeeeeech!' yelped Horrid Henry, gagging and spitting. 'We've been –' cough! '– Dungeon-Drinked!'

And then Horrid Henry heard a horrible sound. Moody Margaret and Sour Susan were outside the Purple Hand Fort. Chanting a victory chant:

'NAH NAH NE NAH NAH!'

EVIL ENEMY

Perfect Peter

KVGVI RH Z HNVOOB GLZW DLIN.

TOP SECRET PHRASE BOOK

Peter is smelly = **Hi!**

Peter is a worm = **Give me all your pocket money.**

Nappy-Face Toad = **I want biscuits.**

Peter is the Duke of Poop = **Goodbye!**

Example:

Peter is smelly. Peter is a worm. Peter is the Duke of Poop.
means
Hi! Give me all your pocket money. Goodbye!

(So I'm NOT calling Peter names. I'm just talking in code.)

MOODY MARGARET
CASTS A SPELL

'**Y**ou are getting sleepy,' said Moody Margaret. 'You are getting very sleepy . . .'

Slowly she waved her watch in front of Susan.

'So sleepy . . . you are now asleep . . . you are now fast asleep . . .'

'No I'm not,' said Sour Susan.

'When I click my fingers you will start snoring.'

Margaret clicked her fingers.

'But I'm not asleep,' said Susan.

Margaret glared at her.

Peter is smelly

'How am I supposed to hypnotise you if you don't try?' said Margaret.

'I *am* trying, you're just a bad hypnotist,' said Susan sourly. 'Now it's my turn.'

'No it's not, it's still mine,' said Margaret.

'You've had your go,' said Susan.

'No I haven't!'

'But I never get to be the hypnotist!' wailed Susan.

'Cry baby!'

'Meanie!'

'Cheater!'

'Cheater!'

Slap!

Slap!

Susan glared at Margaret. Why was

150

she friends with such a mean moody bossyboots?

Margaret glared at Susan. Why was she friends with such a stupid sour sulker?

'I hate you, Margaret!' screamed Sour Susan.

'I hate you more!' screamed Moody Margaret.

'Shut up, landlubbers!' shrieked Horrid Henry from his hammock in the garden next door. 'Or the Purple Hand will make you walk the plank!'

'Shut up yourself, Henry,' said Margaret.

'Yeah, Henry,' said Susan.

'You are stupid, you are stupid,' chanted Rude Ralph, who was playing pirates with Henry.

'You're the stupids,' snapped Moody Margaret. 'Now leave us alone, we're busy.'

'Henry, can I play pirates with you?' asked Perfect Peter, wandering out from the house.

'No, you puny prawn!' screamed

Captain Hook. 'Out of my way before I tear you to pieces with my hook!'

'Muuum,' wailed Peter. 'Henry said he was going to tear me to pieces!'

'Stop being horrid, Henry!' shouted Mum.

'And he won't let me play with him,' said Peter.

'Can't you be nice to your brother for once?' said Dad.

NO! thought Horrid Henry. Why should he be nice to that tell-tale brat?

Horrid Henry did not want to play pirates with Peter. Peter was the world's worst pirate. He couldn't swordfight. He couldn't swashbuckle. He couldn't remember pirate curses. All he could do was whine.

'Okay, Peter, you're the prisoner. Wait in the fort,' said Henry.

'But I'm always the prisoner,' said Peter.

Henry glared at him.

'Do you want to play or don't you?'

'Yes Captain,' said Peter. He crawled into the lair of the Purple Hand. Being prisoner was better than nothing, he supposed. He just hoped he wouldn't have to wait too long.

'Let's get out of here quick,' Henry whispered to Rude Ralph. 'I've got a great idea for playing a trick on Margaret and Susan.' He whispered to Ralph. Ralph grinned.

Horrid Henry hoisted himself onto the low brick wall between his garden and Margaret's.

Moody Margaret was still waving her watch at Susan. Unfortunately, Susan had her back turned and her arms folded.

'Go away, Henry,' ordered Margaret.

'Yeah Henry,' said Susan. 'No boys.'

'Are you being hypnotists?' said Henry.

'Margaret's trying to hypnotise me, only she can't 'cause she's a rubbish hypnotist,' said Susan.

'That's your fault,' said Margaret, glaring.

'Of course you can't hypnotise her,' said Henry. 'You're doing it all wrong.'

'And what would you know about that?' asked Margaret.

'Because,' said Horrid Henry, 'I am a master hypnotist.'

Moody Margaret laughed.

'He is too a master hypnotist,' said Ralph. 'He hypnotises me all the time.'

'Oh yeah?' said Margaret.

'Yeah,' said Henry.

'Prove it,' said Margaret.

'Okay,' said Horrid Henry. 'Gimme the watch.'

Margaret handed it over.

He turned to Ralph.

'Look into my eyes,' he ordered.

Ralph looked into Henry's eyes.

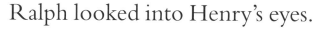

'Now watch the watch,' ordered Henry the hypnotist, swinging the watch back and forth. Rude Ralph swayed.

'You will obey my commands,' said Henry.

'I – will – obey,' said Ralph in a robot voice.

'When I whistle, you will jump off the wall,' said Henry. He whistled.

Ralph jumped off the wall.

'See?' said Horrid Henry.

'That doesn't prove he's hypnotised,' said Margaret. 'You have to make him do silly things.'

'Like what?' said Henry.

'Tell him he's got no clothes on.'

'Ralph, you're a nudie,' said Henry.

Ralph immediately started running round the garden shrieking.

'Aaaaaaarrgghh!' yelped Ralph. 'I'm a nudie! I'm a nudie! Give me some clothes, help help! No one look, I'm naked!'

Margaret hesitated. There was no way Henry could

have *really* hypnotised Ralph – was there?

'I still don't believe he's hypnotised,' said Margaret.

'Then watch this,' said Horrid Henry. 'Ralph – when I snap my fingers you will be . . . Margaret.'

Snap!

'My name is Margaret,' said Ralph. 'I'm a mean bossyboots. I'm the biggest bossiest boot. I'm a frogface.'

Margaret blushed red.

Susan giggled.

'It's not funny,' snapped Margaret. *No one* made fun of her and lived to tell the tale.

'See?' said Henry. 'He obeys my every command.'

'Wow,' said Susan. 'You really are a hypnotist. Can you teach me?'

'Maybe,' said Horrid Henry. 'How much will you pay me?'

'He's just a big faker,' said Margaret. She stuck her nose in the air. 'If you're such a great hypnotist, then hypnotise *me*.'

Oops. Now he was trapped. Margaret was trying to spoil his trick. Well, no way would he let her.

Horrid Henry remembered who he was. The boy who got Miss Battle-Axe sent to the head. The boy who terrified the bogey babysitter. The boy who tricked the Tooth Fairy. He could hypnotise Margaret any day.

'Sure,' he said, waving the watch in front of Margaret.

'You are getting sleepy,' droned Henry. 'You are getting very sleepy. When I snap my fingers you will obey my every command.'

Henry snapped his fingers. Margaret glared at him.

'Well?' said Moody Margaret.

'Don't you know *anything*?' said Horrid Henry. He thought fast. 'That was just the beginning bit. I will complete part two once I have freed Ralph from my power. Ralph, repeat after me, 'I am sellotape'.'

'I am sellotape,' said Rude Ralph. Then he belched.

'I am burping sellotape,' said Rude Ralph. He caught Henry's eye. They burst out laughing.

'Ha ha, Susan, fooled you!' shrieked Henry.

'Did not,' shrieked Susan.

'Did too. Nah nah ne nah nah!' Henry and Ralph ran round Margaret, whooping and cheering.

'Come on Margaret,' said Susan. 'Let's go and do some *real* hypnosis.'

Margaret didn't move.

'Come on, Margaret,' said Susan.

'I am sellotape,' said Margaret.

'No you're not,' said Susan.

'Yes I am,' said Margaret.

Henry and Ralph stopped whooping.

'There's something wrong with Margaret,' said Susan. 'She's acting all funny. Margaret, are you okay? Margaret? Margaret?'

Moody Margaret stood very still. Her eyes looked blank.

Horrid Henry snapped his fingers.

'Raise your right arm,' he ordered.

Margaret raised her right arm.

Huh? thought Horrid Henry.

'Pinch Susan.'

Margaret pinched Susan.

'Owww!' yelped Susan.

'Repeat after me, 'I am a stupid girl'.'

'I am a stupid girl,' said Margaret.

'No you're not,' said Susan.

'Yes I am,' said Margaret.

'She's hypnotised,' said Horrid Henry. He'd actually hypnotised Moody Margaret. This was amazing. This was fantastic. He really truly was a master hypnotist!

'Will you obey me, slave?'

'I will obey,' said Margaret.

'When I click my fingers, you will be a . . . chicken.'

Click!

'Squawk! Squawk! Squawk!' cackled Margaret, flapping her arms wildly.

'What have you done to her?' wailed Sour Susan.

'Wow,' said Rude Ralph. 'You've hypnotised her.'

Horrid Henry could not believe his luck. If he could hypnotise Margaret, he could hypnotise anyone. Everyone would have to obey his commands. He would be master of the world! The universe! Everything!

Henry could see it now.

'Henry, ten out of ten,' Miss Battle-Axe would say. 'Henry is so clever he doesn't ever need to do homework again.'

Oh boy, would he fix Miss Battle-Axe.

He'd make her do the hula in a grass skirt when she wasn't running round the playground mooing like a cow.

He'd make the head, Mrs Oddbod, just have chocolate and cake for school dinners. And no P.E. – ever. In fact, he'd make Mrs Oddbod close down the school.

And as for Mum and Dad . . .

'Henry, have as many sweets as you like,' Dad would say.

'No bedtime for you,' Mum would say.

'Henry, watch as much TV as you want,' Dad would say.

'Henry, here's your pocket money – £1000 a week. Tell us if you need more,' Mum would smile.

'Peter, go to your room and stay there for a year!' Mum and Dad would scream.

Henry would hypnotise them all later. But first, what should he make Margaret do?

Ah yes. Her house was filled with sweets and biscuits and fizzy drinks – all the things Henry's horrible parents never let him have.

'Bring us all your sweets, all your biscuits and a Fizzywizz drink.'

'Yes, master,' said Moody Margaret.

Henry stretched out in the hammock. So did Rude Ralph. This was the life!

Sour Susan didn't know what to do. On the one hand, Margaret was mean and horrible, and she hated her. It was fun watching her obey orders for once. On the other hand, Susan would much rather Margaret was *her* slave than Henry's.

'Unhypnotise her, Henry,' said Sour Susan.

'Soon,' said Horrid Henry.

'Let's hypnotise Peter next,' said Ralph.

'Yeah,' said Henry. No more telling tales. No more goody goody vegetable-eating I'm Mr Perfect. Oh boy would he hypnotise Peter!

Moody Margaret came slowly out of her house. She was carrying a large pitcher and a huge bowl of chocolate mousse.

'Here is your Fizzywizz drink, master,' said

Margaret. Then she poured it on top of him.

'Wha? Wha?' spluttered Henry, gasping and choking.

'And your dinner, frogface,' she added, tipping the mousse all over Ralph.

'Ugggh!' wailed Ralph.

'NAH NAH NE NAH NAH,' shrieked Margaret. 'Fooled you! Fooled you!'

Perfect Peter crept out of the Purple Hand Fort. What was all that yelling? It must be a pirate mutiny!

'Hang on pirates, here I come!' shrieked Peter, charging at the thrashing hammock as fast as he could.

CRASH!

A sopping wet pirate captain and a mousse-covered

first mate lay on the ground. They stared up at their prisoner.

'Hi Henry,' said Peter. 'I mean, hi Captain.' He took a step backwards. 'I mean, Lord High Excellent Majesty.' He took another step back.

'Ugh, we were playing pirate mutiny – weren't we?'

'DIE, WORM!' yelled Horrid Henry, leaping up.

'MUUUUUUM!' shrieked Peter.

Ha ha Henry! Gotcha!
Our dungeon drink trick
was much better than your
stupid stinkbomb.
Nah Nah Ne Nah Nah
The Secret Club rules!

Peter is smelly
Peter is a worm

HOW TO BE A MASTER HYPNOTIST

in 3 easy steps

1 Wave a watch in front of the person you want to hypnotise.

2 Tell them, 'You are getting sleepy. You are getting very sleepy. You are now asleep.'

3 Snap your fingers and order them to be your slave !!!

Z GZIZMGFOZZ GVIVYVXXZ.SZ SZ SZ.

HFHZM SZH KLMTB KZMGH.

Susan has pongy pants.

NZITZIVG RH Z KLGZGL.

Margaret is a potato.

YROO SZH Z YRT SFTV TRMLINLFH YLGGLN.

Bill has a big huge ginormous bottom.

Z GZIZMGFOZ ZGV IVYVXXZ. SZ SZ SZ.

A tarantula ate Rebecca. HA HA HA.

NRHH YZGGOV-ZCV VZGH MRGH.

Miss Battle-Axe eats nits.

HNVOOB GLZW YILGSVIH PVVK LFG.

Smelly toad brothers keep out.

HGVEV RH HGFXP-FK, BFXPB ZMW SLIIRYOV.

Steve is stuck-up, yucky and horrible.

KVGVI RH Z HNVOOB GLZW DLIN.

Peter's a smelly toad worm.

R DZMG Z PROOVI XZGZKFOG ZMW YLN-YLN YZHSVI.

I want a killer catapult and boom-boom basher.

HORRID HENRY AND THE BOGEY BABYSITTER

'No way!' shrieked Tetchy Tess, slamming down the phone.

'No way!' shrieked Crabby Chris, slamming down the phone.

'No way!' shrieked Angry Anna. 'What do you think I am, crazy?'

Even Mellow Martin said he was busy.

Mum hung up the phone and groaned.

It wasn't easy finding someone to babysit more than once for Horrid Henry. When Tetchy Tess came, Henry flooded the bathroom. When Crabby Chris came he hid her homework and 'accidentally' poured red grape juice down the front of her new white jeans. And when Angry Anna came Henry – no, it's too dreadful. Suffice it to say that Anna ran screaming from the house and Henry's parents had to come home early.

Horrid Henry hated babysitters. He wasn't a baby. He didn't want to be sat on. Why should he be nice to some ugly, stuck-up, bossy teenager who'd hog the TV and pig out on Henry's biscuits? Parents should just stay at home where they belonged, thought Horrid Henry.

And now it looked like they would have to. Ha! His parents were mean and horrible, but he'd had a lot of

practice managing them. Babysitters were
unpredictable. Babysitters were hard work. And by
the time you'd broken them in and shown them who
was boss, for some reason they didn't want to come
any more. The only good babysitters let you stay up
all night and eat sweets until you were sick. Sadly,
Horrid Henry never got one of those.

'We have to find a babysitter,' wailed Mum. 'The
party is tomorrow night. I've tried everyone. Who
else is there?'

'There's got to be someone,' said Dad. 'Think!'

Mum thought.

Dad thought.

'What about Rebecca?' said Dad.

Horrid Henry's heart missed a beat. He stopped
drawing moustaches on Perfect Peter's school
pictures. Maybe he'd heard wrong. Oh please, not

Rebecca! Not – Rabid Rebecca!

'Who did you say?' asked Henry. His voice quavered.

'You heard me,' said Dad. 'Rebecca.'

'NO!' screamed Henry. 'She's horrible!'

'She's not horrible,' said Dad. 'She's just – strict.'

'There's no one else,' said Mum grimly. 'I'll phone Rebecca.'

'She's a monster!' wailed Henry. 'She made Ralph go to bed at six o'clock!'

'I like going to bed at six o'clock,' said Perfect Peter. 'After all, growing children need their rest.'

Horrid Henry growled and attacked. He was the Creature from the Black Lagoon, dragging the foolish mortal down to a watery grave.

'AAAEEEEE!' squealed Peter. 'Henry pulled my hair.'

'Stop being horrid, Henry!' said Dad. 'Mum's on the phone.'

Henry prayed. Maybe she'd be busy. Maybe she'd say no. Maybe she'd be dead. He'd heard all about Rebecca. She'd made Tough Toby get in his pyjamas at five o'clock *and* do all his homework. She'd unplugged Dizzy Dave's computer. She'd made Moody Margaret wash the floor. No doubt about it, Rabid Rebecca was the toughest teen in town.

Henry lay on the rug and howled. Mum shouted into the phone.

'You can! That's great, Rebecca. No, that's just the TV – sorry for the noise. See you tomorrow.'

'NOOOOOOOOOO!' wailed Henry.

Ding dong.

'I'll get it!' said Perfect Peter. He skipped to the door.

Henry flung himself on the carpet.

'I DON'T WANT TO HAVE A BABYSITTER!' he wailed.

The door opened. In walked the biggest, meanest, ugliest, nastiest-looking girl Henry had ever seen. Her arms were enormous. Her head was enormous. Her teeth were enormous. She looked like she ate elephants for breakfasts, crocodiles for lunch, and snacked on toddlers for tea.

'What have you got to eat?' snarled Rabid Rebecca.

Dad took a step back. 'Help yourself to anything in the fridge,' said Dad.

'Don't worry, I will,' said Rebecca.

'GO HOME, YOU WITCH!' howled Henry.

'Bedtime is nine o'clock,' shouted Dad, trying to be heard above Henry's screams. He edged his way carefully past Rebecca, jumped over Henry, then dashed out the front door.

'I DON'T WANT TO HAVE A BABYSITTER!' shrieked Henry.

'Be good, Henry,' said Mum weakly. She stepped

over Henry, then escaped from the house.

The door closed.

Horrid Henry was alone in the house with Rabid
Rebecca.

He glared at Rebecca.

Rebecca glared at him.

'I've heard all about you, you little creep,' growled
Rebecca. 'No one bothers me when I'm babysitting.'

Horrid Henry stopped screaming.

'Oh yeah,' said Horrid Henry. 'We'll see about
that.'

Rabid Rebecca bared her fangs. Henry recoiled.
Perhaps I'd better keep out of her way, he thought,
then slipped into the sitting room and turned on the
telly.

Ahh, Mutant Max. Hurray! How bad could life be when a brilliant programme like Mutant Max was on? He'd annoy Rebecca as soon as it was over.

Rebecca stomped into the room and snatched the clicker.

ZAP!

DA DOO, DA DOO DA, DA DOO DA DOO DA, tangoed some horrible spangly dancers.

'Hey,' said Henry. 'I'm watching Mutant Max.'

'Tough,' said Rebecca. '*I'm* watching ballroom dancing.'

Snatch!

Horrid Henry grabbed the clicker.

ZAP!

'And it's mutants, mutants, mut – '

Snatch!

Zap!

DA DOO, DA DOO DA, DA DOO DA DOODA. DOO, DA DOO DA, DA DOO DA DOO DA.

Horrid Henry tangoed round the room, gliding and sliding.

'Stop it,' muttered Rebecca.

Henry shimmied back and forth in front of the telly, blocking her view and singing along as loudly as he could.

'DA DOO, DA DOO DA,' warbled Henry.

'I'm warning you,' hissed Rebecca.

Perfect Peter walked in. He had already put on his blue bunny pyjamas, brushed his teeth and combed his hair. He held a game of Chinese Checkers in his hand.

'Rebecca, will you play a game with me before I go to bed?' asked Peter.

'NO!' roared Rebecca. 'I'm trying to watch TV. Shut up and go away.'

Perfect Peter leapt back.

'But I thought – since I was all ready for bed – he stammered.

'I've got better things to do than to play with you,' snarled Rebecca. 'Now go to bed this minute, both of you.'

'But it's not my bedtime for hours,' protested Henry. 'I want to watch Mutant Max.'

'Nor mine,' said Perfect Peter timidly. 'There's this nature programme –'

'GO!' howled Rebecca.

'NO!' howled Henry.

'RAAAAA!' roared Rabid Rebecca.

Horrid Henry did not know how it happened. It was as if fiery dragon's breath had blasted him upstairs. Somehow, he was in his pyjamas, in bed, and it was only seven o'clock.

Nappy-Face Toad

Rabid Rebecca switched off the light. 'Don't even think of moving from that bed,' she hissed. 'If I see you, or hear you, or even smell you, you'll be sorry you were born. I'll stay downstairs, you stay upstairs, and that way no one will get hurt.' Then she marched out of the room and slammed the door.

Horrid Henry was so shocked he could not move. He, Horrid Henry, the bulldozer of babysitters, the terror of teachers, the bully of brothers, was in bed, lights out, at seven o'clock.

Seven o'clock! Two whole hours before his bedtime! This was an outrage! He could hear Moody Margaret shrieking next door. He could hear Toddler Tom zooming about on his tricycle. No one went to bed at seven o'clock. Not even toddlers!

Worst of all, he was thirsty. So what if

she told me to stay in bed, thought Horrid Henry. I'm thirsty. I'm going to go downstairs and get myself a glass of water. It's my house and I'll do what I want.

Horrid Henry did not move.

I'm dying of thirst here, thought Henry. Mum and Dad will come home and I'll be a dried out old stick insect, and boy will she be in trouble.

Horrid Henry still did not move.

Go on, feet, urged Henry, let's just step on down and get a little ol' glass of water. So what if that bogey babysitter said he had to stay in bed. What could she do to him?

She could chop off my
head and bounce it down
the stairs, thought Henry.

Eeek.

Well, let her try.

Horrid Henry
remembered who he
was. The boy who'd sent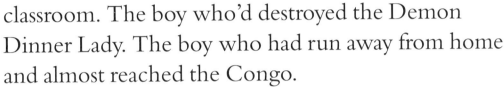
teachers shrieking from the
classroom. The boy who'd destroyed the Demon
Dinner Lady. The boy who had run away from home
and almost reached the Congo.

I will get up and get a drink of water, he thought.

Horrid Henry crept to the
bedroom door.

Slowly he opened it a crack.

Creak.

Then slowly, slowly, he opened
the door a bit more and slipped out.

ARGHHHHHH!

There was Rabid Rebecca sitting
at the top of the stairs.

It's a trap, thought Henry. She was lying in wait for me. I'm dead, I'm finished, they'll find my bones in the morning.

Horrid Henry dashed back inside his room and awaited his doom.

Silence.

What was going on? Why hadn't Rebecca torn him apart limb from limb?

Horrid Henry opened his door a fraction and peeped out.

Rabid Rebecca was still sitting huddled at the top of the stairs. She did not move. Her eyes were fixed straight ahead.

'Spi–spi–spider,' she whispered. She pointed at a big, hairy spider in front of her with a trembling hand.

'It's huge,' said Henry. 'Really hairy and horrible and wriggly and –'

'STOP!' squealed Rebecca. 'Help me, Henry,' she begged.

Horrid Henry was not the fearless leader of a pirate

gang for nothing.

'If I risk my life and get rid of the spider, can I watch Mutant Max?' said Henry.

'Yes,' said Rebecca.

'And stay up till my parents come home?'

'Yes,' said Rebecca.

'And eat all the ice cream in the fridge?'

'YES!' shrieked Rebecca. 'Just get rid of that – that –'

'Deal,' said Horrid Henry.

He dashed to his room and grabbed a jar.

Rabid Rebecca hid her eyes as Horrid Henry scooped up the spider. What a beauty!

'It's gone,' said Henry.

Rebecca opened her beady red eyes.

'Right, back to bed, you little brat!'

'What?' said Henry.

'Bed. Now!' screeched Rebecca.

'But we agreed . . .' said Henry.

'Tough,' said Rebecca. 'That was then.'

'Traitor,' said Henry.

He whipped out the spider jar from behind his back and unscrewed the lid.

'On guard!' he said.

'AAEEEE!' whimpered Rebecca.

Horrid Henry advanced menacingly towards her.

'NOOOOOOO!' wailed Rebecca, stepping back.

'Now get in that room and stay there,' ordered Henry. 'Or else.'

Rabid Rebecca skedaddled into the bathroom and locked the door.

'If I see you or hear you or even smell you you'll be sorry you were born,' said Henry.

'I already am,' said Rabid Rebecca.

Horrid Henry spent a lovely evening in front of the telly. He watched scary movies. He ate ice cream and sweets and biscuits and crisps until he could stuff no more in.

Vroom vroom.

Oops. Parents home.

Horrid Henry dashed upstairs and leapt into bed just as the front door opened.

Mum and Dad looked around the sitting room, littered with sweet wrappers, biscuit crumbs and ice cream cartons.

'You did tell her to help herself,' said Mum.

'Still,' said Dad. 'What a pig.'

'Never mind,' said Mum brightly, 'at least she managed to get Henry to bed. That's a first.'

Rabid Rebecca staggered into the room.

'Did you get enough to eat?' said Dad.

'No,' said Rabid Rebecca.

'Oh,' said Dad.

'Was everything all right?' asked Mum.

Rebecca looked at her.

'Can I go now?' said Rebecca.

'Any chance you could babysit on Saturday?' asked Dad hopefully.

'What do you think I am, crazy?' shrieked Rebecca.

SLAM!

Upstairs, Horrid Henry groaned.

Rats. It was so unfair. Just when he had a babysitter beautifully trained, for some reason they wouldn't come back.

EVIL ENEMY

Rabid Rebecca

EVIL ENEMIES FACT FILE

Worst enemies

Peter
Nickname: Perfect
Worst features:
too many to count
Best feature: none
Most evil crime:
being born

Margaret
Nickname: Moody
Worst features:
grouchy, bossy
Best feature: owns a
pirate hook, sabre and
cutlass
Most evil crime:
living next door

Susan

Nickname: Sour

Worst feature: whining, moaning copycat

Best feature: slaps Margaret

Most evil crime: joining Margaret's secret club

Steve

Nickname: Stuck-up

Worst feature: always bragging about how rich he is

Best feature: lives far away

Most evil crime: trying to trick me into thinking his house was haunted

Bill
Nickname: Bossy
Worst feature: mean, double-crossing creep
Best feature: doesn't go to my school
Most evil crime: getting me into trouble at Dad's office

Rebecca
Nickname: Rabid
Worst features: toughest teen in town. Makes children go to bed early and hogs the TV.
Best feature: scared of spiders
Most evil crime: making me go to bed at 7 pm!!

Lily

Nickname: Lisping
Worst feature: follows me around
Best feature: smaller than me
Most evil crime: asking me to marry her

Worst babysitters

Tetchy Tess
Crabby Chris
Angry Anna
Rabid Rebecca

Other things I hate

Homework
Boring holidays
Walks
Fresh air
Healthy food
Bedtime

Greatest victories

Tricking Bossy Bill into photocopying his bottom
Switching Christmas presents with Stuck-up Steve
Stinkbombing Moody Margaret's Secret Club
Enlisting Sour Susan as a double agent
Defeating Rabid Rebecca
Escaping Lisping Lily
Being older, bigger and cleverer than Perfect Peter

Peter is the Duke of Poop

HORRID HENRY'S YEAR BOOK

Our Christmas Play

The Queen's Visit

The Big
Football Match

Our School
Band

Tidy Monitors

HORRID HENRY'S INJECTION

AAGGH!!
AAAAGGGHHH!!!!
AAAAAGGGGGHHHHHH!!!!

The horrible screams came from behind Nurse
Needle's closed door.

Horrid Henry looked at his younger brother
Perfect Peter. Perfect Peter looked at Horrid Henry.
Then they both looked at their father, who
stared straight ahead.

Henry and Peter were in
Dr Dettol's waiting room.

Moody Margaret was there.
So were Sour Susan, Anxious
Andrew, Jolly Josh, Weepy
William, Tough Toby, Lazy
Linda, Clever Clare, Rude
Ralph and just about everyone
Henry knew. They were all waiting for the terrible
moment when Nurse Needle would call their name.

Today was the worst day in the world. Today was –
injection day.

Horrid Henry was not afraid of spiders.

He was not afraid of spooks.

He was not afraid of burglars, bad dreams, squeaky

doors and things that go bump in the night. Only one thing scared him.

Just thinking about . . . about . . . Henry could barely even say the word – INJECTIONS – made him shiver and quiver and shake and quake.

Nurse Needle came into the waiting room.

Henry held his breath.

'Please let it be someone else,' he prayed.

'William!' said Nurse Needle.

Weepy William burst into tears.

'Let's have none of that,' said Nurse Needle. She took him firmly by the arm and closed the door behind him.

'I don't need an injection!' said Henry. 'I feel fine.'

'Injections stop you getting ill,' said Dad. 'Injections fight germs.'

'I don't believe in germs,' said Henry.

'I do,' said Dad.

'I do,' said Peter.

'Well, I don't,' said Henry.

Dad sighed. 'You're having an injection, and that's that.'

'I don't mind injections,' said Perfect Peter. 'I know how good they are for me.'

Horrid Henry pretended he was an alien who'd come from outer space to jab earthlings.

'OWW!' shrieked Peter.

'Don't be horrid, Henry!' shouted Dad.

AAAAAAGGGGGGHHHHHHH!

came the terrible screams from behind Nurse Needle's door.

AAAAAAGGGGGGHHHHHHH!
NOOOOO O O O!

Then Weepy William staggered out, clutching his arm and wailing.

'Crybaby,' said Henry.

'Just wait, Henry,' sobbed William.

Nurse Needle came into the waiting room.

Henry closed his eyes.

'Don't pick me,' he begged silently. 'Don't pick me.'

'Susan!' said Nurse Needle.

Sour Susan crept into Nurse Needle's office.

AAAAAAGGGGGHHHHHH!

came the terrible screams.

AAAAAAGGGGGGHHHHHHH!
NOOOOO O O O!

Then Sour Susan dragged herself out, clutching her arm and snivelling.

'What a crybaby,' said Henry.

'Well, we all know about *you*, Henry,' said Susan sourly.

'Oh yeah?' said Henry. 'You don't know anything.'

Nurse Needle reappeared.

Henry hid his face behind his hands.

I'll be so good if it's not me, he thought. Please, let it be someone else.

'Margaret!' said Nurse Needle.

Henry relaxed.

'Hey, Margaret, did you know the needles are so big and sharp they can go right through your arm?' said Henry.

Moody Margaret ignored him and marched into Nurse Needle's office.

Henry could hardly wait for her terrible screams. Boy, would he tease that crybaby Margaret!

Silence.

Then Moody Margaret swaggered into the waiting room, proudly displaying an enormous plaster on her arm. She smiled at Henry.

'Ooh, Henry, you won't believe the needle she's using today,' said Margaret. 'It's as long as my leg.'

'Shut up, Margaret,' said Henry. He was breathing very fast and felt faint.

'Anything wrong, Henry?' asked Margaret sweetly.

'No,' said Henry. He scowled at her. How dare she not scream and cry?

'Oh, good,' said Margaret. 'I just wanted to warn you because I've never seen such big fat whopping needles in all my life!'

Horrid Henry steadied himself. Today would be different.

He would be brave.

He would be fearless.

He would march into Nurse Needle's office, offer his arm, and dare her to do her worst. Yes, today was the day. Brave Henry, he would be called, the boy who laughed when the needle went in, the boy who asked for a second injection, the boy who –

'Henry!' said Nurse Needle.

'NO!' shrieked Henry.

'Please, please, NO!'

'Yes,' said Nurse Needle. 'It's your turn now.'

Henry forgot he was brave.

Henry forgot he was fearless.

Henry forgot everyone was watching him.

Henry started screaming and screeching and kicking.

'OW!' yelped Dad.

'OW!' yelped Perfect Peter.

'OW!' yelped Lazy Linda.

Then everyone started screaming and screeching.

'I don't want an injection!' shrieked Horrid Henry.

'I don't want an injection!' shrieked Anxious Andrew.

'I don't want an injection!' shrieked Tough Toby.

'Stop it,' said Nurse Needle. 'You need an injection and an injection is what you will get.'

'Him first!' screamed Henry, pointing at Peter.

'You're such a baby, Henry,' said Clever Clare.

That did it.

No one *ever* called Henry a baby and lived.

He kicked Clare as hard as he could. Clare screamed.

Nurse Needle and Dad each grabbed one of Henry's arms and dragged him howling into her office. Peter followed behind, whistling softly.

Henry wriggled free and dashed out. Dad nabbed him and brought him back. Nurse Needle's door clanged shut behind them.

Henry stood in the corner. He was trapped.

Nurse Needle kept her distance. Nurse Needle knew Henry. Last time he'd had an injection he'd kicked her.

Dr Dettol came in.

'What's the trouble, Nurse?' she asked.

'Him,' said Nurse Needle. 'He doesn't want an injection.'

Dr Dettol kept her distance. Dr Dettol knew Henry. Last time he'd had an injection he'd bitten her.

'Take a seat, Henry,' said Dr Dettol.

Henry collapsed in a chair. There was no escape.

'What a fuss over a little thing like an injection,' said Dr Dettol. 'Call me if you need me,' she added, and left the room.

Henry sat on the chair, breathing hard. He tried not

to look as Nurse
Needle examined
her gigantic pile
of syringes.

But he could not
stop himself peeking
through his fingers.
He watched as she got
the injection ready,
choosing the longest,
sharpest, most wicked
needle Henry had ever
seen.

Then Nurse Needle approached, weapon in hand.

'Him first!' shrieked Henry.

Perfect Peter sat down and rolled up his sleeve.

'I'll go first,' said Peter. 'I don't mind.'

'Oh,' he said, as he was jabbed.

'That was perfect,' said Nurse Needle.

'What a good boy you are,' said Dad.

Perfect Peter smiled proudly.

Nurse Needle rearmed herself.

Horrid Henry shrank back in the chair. He looked
around wildly.

Then Henry noticed the row of little medicine
bottles lined up on the counter. Nurse Needle was
filling her syringes from them.

Henry looked closer. The labels read: 'Do NOT give injection if a child is feverish or seems ill.'

Nurse Needle came closer, brandishing the injection. Henry coughed.

And closer. Henry sneezed.

And closer. Henry wheezed and rasped and panted.

Nurse Needle lowered her arm.

'Are you all right, Henry?'

'No,' gasped Henry. 'I'm ill. My chest hurts, my head hurts, my throat hurts.'

Nurse Needle felt his sweaty forehead.

Henry coughed again, a dreadful throaty cough.

'I can't breathe,' he choked. 'Asthma.'

'You don't have asthma, Henry,' said Dad.

'I do, too,' said Henry, gasping for breath.

Nurse Needle frowned.

'He is a little warm,' she said.

'I'm ill,' whispered Henry pathetically. 'I feel terrible.'

Nurse Needle put down her syringe.

'I think you'd better bring him back when he's feeling better,' she said.

'All right,' said Dad. He'd make sure Henry's mother brought him next time.

Henry wheezed and sneezed, moaned and groaned, all the way home. His parents put him straight to bed.

'Oh, Mum,' said Henry, trying to sound as weak as possible. 'Could you bring me some chocolate ice cream to soothe my throat? It really hurts.'

'Of course,' said Mum. 'You poor boy.'

Henry snuggled down in the cool sheets. Ahh, this was the life.

'Oh, Mum,' added Henry, coughing. 'Could you bring up the TV? Just in case my head stops hurting long enough for me to watch?'

'Of course,' said Mum.

Boy, this was great! thought Henry. No injection! No school tomorrow! Supper in bed!

There was a knock on the door. It must be Mum with his ice cream. Henry sat up in bed, then remembered he was ill. He lay back and closed his eyes.

'Come in, Mum,' said Henry hoarsely.

'Hello, Henry.'

Henry opened his eye. It wasn't Mum. It was Dr Dettol.

Henry closed his eyes and had a terrible coughing fit.

'What hurts?' said Dr Dettol.

'Everything,' said Henry. 'My head, my throat, my chest, my eyes, my ears, my back and my legs.'

'Oh dear,' said Dr Dettol.

She took out her stethoscope and listened to Henry's chest. All clear.

She stuck a little stick in his mouth and told him to say 'AAAAAH.' All clear.

She examined his eyes and ears, his back and his
legs. Everything seemed fine.

'Well, doctor?' said Mum.

Dr Dettol shook her head. She looked grave.

'He's very ill,' said Dr Dettol. 'There's only one
cure.'

'What?' said Mum.

'What?' said Dad.

'An injection!'

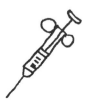

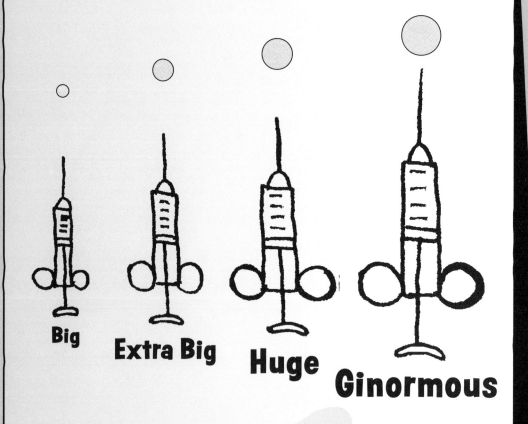

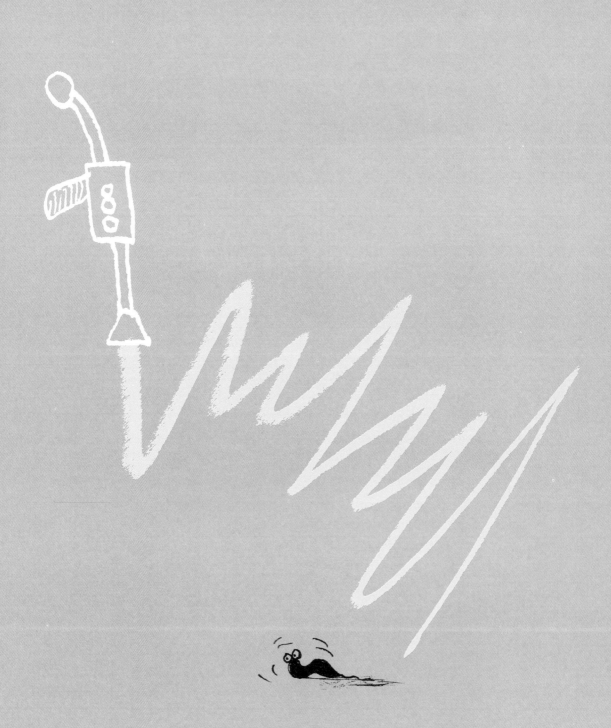

HORRID HENRY'S SCHOOL FAIR

'enry! Peter! I need your donations to the school fair NOW!'

Mum was in a bad mood. She was helping Moody Margaret's mum organise the fair and had been nagging Henry for ages to give away some of his old games and toys. Horrid Henry hated giving. He liked getting.

Horrid Henry stood in his bedroom. Everything he owned was on the floor.

'How about giving away those bricks?' said Mum. 'You never play with them any more.'

'NO!' said Henry. They were bound to come in useful some day.

'How about some soft toys? When was the last time you played with Spotty Dog?'

'NO!' said Horrid Henry. 'He's mine!'

Perfect Peter appeared in the doorway dragging two enormous sacks.

'Here's my contribution to the school fair, Mum,' said Perfect Peter.

Mum peeped inside the bags.

'Are you sure you want to give away so many toys?' said Mum.

'Yes,' said Peter. 'I'd like other children to have fun playing with them.'

'What a generous boy you are, Peter,' she said, giving him a big hug.

Henry scowled. Peter could give away all his toys, for all Henry cared. Henry wanted to keep everything.

Wait! How could he have forgotten?

Henry reached under his bed and pulled out a large box hidden under a blanket. The box contained all the useless, horrible presents Henry had ever received. Packs of hankies. Vests with ducks on them. A nature guide. Uggh! Henry hated nature. Why would anyone want to waste their time looking at pictures of flowers and trees?

And then, right at the bottom, was the worst present of all. A Walkie-Talkie-Burpy-Slurpy-Teasy-Weasy Doll. He'd got it for Christmas from a great-aunt he'd never met. The card she'd written was still attached.

Dear Henrietta
I thought this doll would be perfect for a sweet little two-year-old like you! Take good care of your new baby!
Love
Great-Aunt Greta

Even worse, she'd sent Peter something brilliant.

Dear Pete
You must be a teenager by now and too old for toys, so here's £25. Don't spend it all on sweets!
Love
Great-Aunt Greta

Henry had screamed and begged, but Peter got to keep the money, and Henry was stuck with the doll. He was far too embarrassed to try to sell it, so the doll just lived hidden under his bed with all the other rotten gifts.

'Take that,' said Henry, giving the doll a kick.

'Mama Mama Mama!' burbled the doll. 'Baby burp!'

'Not Great-Aunt Greta's present!' said Mum.

'Take it or leave it,' said Henry. 'You can have the rest as well.'

Mum sighed. 'Some lucky children are going to be very happy.' She took the hateful presents and put them in the jumble sack.

Phew! He'd got rid of that doll at last! He'd lived in terror of Rude Ralph or Moody Margaret coming over and finding it. Now he'd never have to see that burping slurping long-haired thing again.

Henry crept into the spare room where Mum was keeping all the donated toys and games for the fair. He thought he'd have a quick poke around and see what good stuff would be for sale tomorrow. That way he could make a dash and be first in the queue.

There were rolls of raffle tickets, bottles of wine, the barrel for the lucky dip, and sacks and sacks of toys. Wow, what a hoard! Henry just had to move that rolled-up poster out of the way and start rummaging!

Henry pushed aside the poster and then stopped.

I wonder what this is, he thought. I think I'll just unroll it and have a little peek. No harm in that.

Carefully, he untied the ribbon and laid the poster flat on the floor. Then he gasped.

This wasn't jumble. It was the Treasure Map! Whoever guessed where the treasure was hidden always won a fabulous prize. Last year Sour Susan had won a skateboard. The year before Jolly Josh had won a Super Soaker 2000. Boy it sure was worth trying to find that treasure! Horrid Henry usually had at least five goes. But his luck was so bad he had never even come close.

Henry looked at the map. There was the island, with its caves and lagoons, and the sea surrounding it,

filled with whales and sharks and pirate ships. The map was divided into a hundred numbered squares. Somewhere under one of those squares was an X.

I'll just admire the lovely picture, thought Henry. He stared and stared. No X. He ran his hands over the map. No X.

Henry sighed. It was so unfair! He never won anything. And this year the prize was sure to be a Super Soaker 5000.

Henry lifted the map to roll it up. As he raised the thick paper to the light, a large, unmistakable X was suddenly visible beneath square 42.

The treasure was just under the whale's eye.

He had discovered the secret.

'YES!' said Horrid Henry, punching the air. 'It's my lucky day, at last!'

But wait. Mum was in charge of the Treasure Map stall. If he was first in the queue and instantly bagged square 42 she was sure to be suspicious. So how could he let a few other children go first, but make sure none of them chose the right square? And then suddenly, he had a brilliant, spectacular idea . . .

'Tra la la la la!' trilled Horrid Henry, as he, Peter, Mum and Dad walked to the school fair.

'You're cheerful today, Henry,' said Dad.

'I'm feeling lucky,' said Horrid Henry.

He burst into the playground and went straight to the Treasure Map stall. A large queue of eager children keen to pay 20p for a chance to guess had already formed. There was the mystery prize, a large, tempting, Super Soaker–sized box. Wheeee!

Rude Ralph was first in line.

'Psst, Ralph,' whispered Henry. 'I know where X marks the spot. I'll tell you if you give me 50p.'

'Deal,' said Ralph.

'92,' whispered Henry.

'Thanks!' said Ralph. He wrote his name in square 92 and walked off, whistling.

Moody Margaret was next.

'Pssst, Margaret,' whispered Henry. 'I know where X marks the spot.'

'Where?' said Margaret.

'Pay me 50p and I'll tell you,' whispered Henry.

'Why should I trust you?' said Margaret loudly.

Henry shrugged.

'Don't trust me then, and I'll tell Susan,' said Henry.

Margaret gave Henry 50p.

'2,' whispered Horrid Henry.

Margaret wrote her name in square 2, and skipped off.

Henry told Lazy Linda the treasure square was 4.

Henry told Dizzy Dave the treasure square was 100.

Weepy William was told 22.

Anxious Andrew was told 14.

Then Henry thought it was time he bagged the winning square. He made sure none of the children he'd tricked were nearby, then pushed into the queue behind Beefy Bert. His pockets bulged with cash.

'What number do you want, Bert?' asked Henry's mum.

'I dunno,' said Bert.

'Hi Mum,' said Henry. 'Here's my 20p. Hmmm, now where could that treasure be?'

Horrid Henry pretended to study the map.

'I think I'll try 37,' he said. 'No wait, 84. Wait, wait, I'm still deciding . . .'

'Hurry up Henry,' said Mum. 'Other children want to have a go.'

'Okay, 42,' said Henry.

Mum looked at him. Henry smiled at her and wrote his name in the square.

Then he sauntered off.

He could feel that Super Soaker in his hands already. Wouldn't it be fun to spray the teachers!

Horrid Henry had a fabulous day. He threw wet sponges at Miss Battle-Axe in the 'Biff a Teacher' stall. He joined in his class square dance. He got a marble in the lucky dip. Henry didn't even scream when Perfect Peter won a box of notelets in the raffle and Henry didn't win anything, despite spending £3 on tickets.

TIME TO FIND THE WINNER OF THE TREASURE MAP COMPETITION

boomed a voice over the playground.

Everyone stampeded to the stall.

Suddenly Henry had a terrible thought. What if Mum had switched the X to a different spot at the last minute? He couldn't bear it. He absolutely couldn't bear it. He had to have that Super Soaker!

'And the winning number is . . .' Mum lifted up the Treasure Map . . . '42! The winner is – Henry.'

'Yes!' screamed Henry.

'What?' screamed Rude Ralph, Moody Margaret, Lazy Linda, Weepy William, and Anxious Andrew.

'Here's your prize, Henry,' said Mum.

She handed Henry the enormous box.

'Congratulations.' She did not look very pleased.

Eagerly, Henry tore off the wrapping paper. His prize was a Walkie-Talkie-Burpy-Slurpy-Teasy-Weasy Doll.

'Mama Mama Mama!' burbled the doll. 'Baby Slurp!'

AAARRGGGHHHH!

howled Henry.

Horrid Henry has lost 5 knights, Mr Kill and his Goo-Shooter. Can you find them?

HORRID HENRY'S DANCE CLASS

Stomp stomp stomp
stompstompstompstomp.

Horrid Henry was practising his elephant dance.

Tap tap tap tap tap tap tap tap.

Perfect Peter was practising his raindrop dance. Peter was practising being a raindrop for his dance class show.

Henry was also supposed to be practising being a raindrop. But Henry did not want to be a raindrop. He did not want to be a tomato, a string bean, or a banana either.

Stomp stomp stomp

went Henry's heavy boots.

Tap tap tap

went Peter's tap shoes.

226

'You're doing it wrong, Henry,' said Peter.

'No I'm not,' said Henry.

'You are too,' said Peter. 'We're supposed to be raindrops.'

Stomp stomp stomp

went Henry's boots. He was an elephant smashing his way through the jungle, trampling on everyone who stood in his way.

'I can't concentrate with you stomping,' said Peter. 'And I have to practise my solo.'

'Who cares?' screamed Horrid Henry. 'I hate dancing, I hate dance class, and most of all, I hate you!'

This was not entirely true. Horrid Henry loved dancing. Henry danced in his bedroom. Henry danced

up and down the stairs. Henry danced on the new sofa
and on the kitchen table.

What Henry hated was having to dance
with other children.

'Couldn't I go to karate instead?' asked
Henry every Saturday.

'No,' said Mum. 'Too violent.'

'Judo?' said Henry.

'N–O spells no,' said Dad.

So every Saturday
morning at 9.45,
Henry and Peter's
father drove them to
Miss Impatience Tutu's
Dance Studio.

Miss Impatience Tutu was skinny and bony. She had long stringy grey hair. Her nose was sharp. Her elbows were pointy. Her knees were wobbly. No one had ever seen her smile.

Perhaps this was because Impatience Tutu hated teaching.

Impatience Tutu hated noise.

Impatience Tutu hated children.

But most of all Impatience Tutu hated Horrid Henry.

This was not surprising. When Miss Tutu shouted, 'Class, lift your left legs,' eleven left legs lifted. One right leg sagged to the floor.

When Miss Tutu screamed, 'Heel, toe, heel, toe,' eleven dainty feet tapped away. One clumpy foot stomped toe, heel, toe, heel.

When Miss Tutu bellowed, 'Class, skip to your right,' eleven bodies turned to the right. One body galumphed to the left.

Naturally, no one wanted to dance with Henry. Or indeed, anywhere near Henry. Today's class, unfortunately, was no different.

'Miss Tutu, Henry is treading on my toes,' said Jolly Josh.

'Miss Tutu, Henry is kicking my legs,' said Lazy Linda.

'Miss Tutu, Henry is bumping me,' said Vain Violet.

'HENRY!' screeched Miss Tutu.

'Yeah,' said Henry.

'I am a patient woman, and you are trying my patience to the limit,' hissed Miss Tutu. 'Any more bad behaviour and you will be very sorry.'

'What will happen?' asked Horrid Henry eagerly.

Miss Tutu stood very tall. She took a long, bony finger and dragged it slowly across her throat.

Henry decided that he would rather live to do battle another day. He stood on the side, gnashing his teeth, pretending he was an enormous crocodile about to gobble up Miss Tutu.

'This is our final rehearsal before the show,' barked Miss Tutu. 'Everything must be perfect.'

Eleven faces stared at Miss Tutu. One face scowled at the floor.

'Tomatoes and beans to the front,' ordered Miss Tutu.

'When Miss Thumper plays the music everyone will

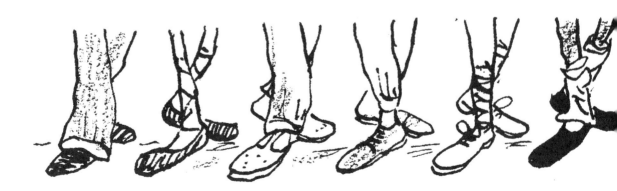

stretch out their arms to the
sky, to kiss the morning hello.
Raindrops, stand at the back
next to the giant green leaves
and wait until the beans find the
magic bananas. And Henry,' spat
Miss Tutu, glaring. 'TRY to get
it right.

'Positions, everybody. Miss Thumper,
the opening music please!'
shouted Miss Tutu.
Miss Thumper
banged away.
The tomatoes weaved in
and out, twirling.
The beans pirouetted.
The bananas pointed their
toes and swayed.
The raindrops pitter-patted.

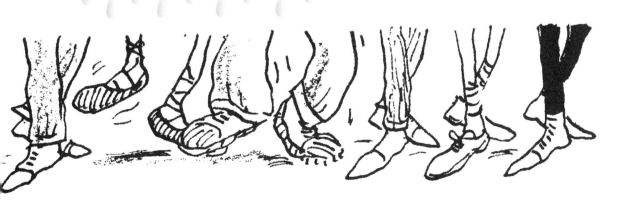

All except one. Henry waved his arms frantically and
raced round the room. Then he crashed into the beans.

'HENRY!' screeched Miss Tutu.

'Yeah,' scowled Henry.

'Sit in the corner!'

Henry was delighted. He sat in the corner and made horrible rude faces while Peter did his raindrop solo.

Tap tap tap tap tap tap tap. Tappa tappa tappa tappa tap tap tap. Tappa tip tappa tip tappa tappa tappa tip.

'Was that perfect, Miss Tutu?' asked Peter.

Miss Tutu sighed. 'Perfect, Peter, as always,' she said, and the corner of her mouth trembled slightly. This was the closest Miss Tutu ever came to smiling.

Then she saw Henry slouching on the chair. Her mouth drooped back into its normal grim position.

Miss Tutu tugged Henry off the chair. She shoved him to the very back of the stage, behind the other raindrops. Then she pushed him behind a giant green leaf.

'Stand there!' shouted Miss Tutu.

'But no one will see me here,' said Henry.

'Precisely,' said Miss Tutu.

It was showtime.

The curtain was about to rise.

The children stood quietly on stage.

Perfect Peter was so excited he almost bounced up and down. Naturally he controlled himself and stood still.

233

Horrid Henry was not very excited.

He did not want to be a raindrop.

And he certainly did not want to be a raindrop who danced behind a giant green leaf.

Miss Thumper waddled over to the piano. She banged on the keys.

The curtain went up.

Henry's mum and dad were in the audience with the other parents. As usual they sat in the back row, in case they had to make a quick getaway.

They smiled and waved at Peter, standing proudly at the front.

'Can you see Henry?' whispered Henry's mum.

Henry's dad squinted at the stage.

A tuft of red hair stuck up behind the green leaf.

'I think that's him behind the leaf,' said his father doubtfully.

'I wonder why Henry is hiding,' said Mum. 'It's not like him to be shy.'

'Hmmmm,' said Dad.

'Shhh,' hissed the parents beside them.

Henry watched the tomatoes and beans searching on tiptoe for the magic bananas.

I'm not staying back here, he thought, and pushed his way through the raindrops.

'Stop pushing, Henry!' hissed Lazy Linda.

Henry pushed harder, then did a few pitter-pats with the other raindrops.

Miss Tutu stretched out a bony arm and yanked Henry back behind the scenery.

Who wants to be a raindrop anyway, thought Henry. I can do what I like hidden here.

The tomatoes weaved in and out, twirling.

The beans pirouetted.

The bananas pointed their toes and swayed.

The raindrops pitter-patted.

Henry flapped his arms and pretended he was a pterodactyl about to pounce on Miss Tutu.

Round and round he flew, homing in on his prey.

236

Perfect Peter stepped to the front and began his solo.

Tap tap tap tap

tap tap –

cRASH!

One giant green leaf fell on top of the raindrops, knocking them over.

The raindrops collided with the tomatoes.

The tomatoes smashed into the string beans.

The string beans bumped into the bananas.

Perfect Peter turned his head to see what was happening and danced off the stage into the front row.

Miss Tutu fainted.

The only person still standing on stage was Henry.

Stomp stomp stomp stompstompstompstomp.

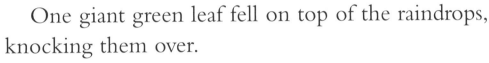

Henry did his elephant dance.

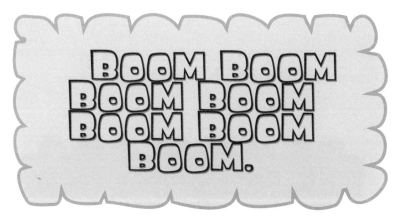

BOOM BOOM BOOM BOOM BOOM BOOM BOOM.

Henry did his buffalo dance.
Peter tried to scramble back on stage.

The curtain fell.

There was a long silence, then Henry's parents clapped.

No one else did, so Henry's parents stopped.

All the other parents ran up to Miss Tutu and started shouting.

'I don't see why that horrid boy should have had such a long solo while all Linda did was lie on the floor,' yelled one mother.

'My Josh is a much better dancer than that boy,' shouted another. 'He should have done the solo.'

'I didn't know you taught modern dance, Miss Tutu,' said Violet's mother. 'Come, Violet,' she added, sweeping from the room.

'HENRY!!' screeched Miss Tutu. 'Leave my dance studio at once!'

'Whoopee!' shouted Henry. He knew that next Saturday he would be at karate class at last.

DON'T MISS THE DANCE EVENT OF THE YEAR!

MISS IMPATIENCE TUTU AND HER TUTURETTES
will be dancing in the world premiere of

THE FARMER'S MARKET

See beans and tomatoes do the Vegetable Waltz!
Marvel at the Plum Fairy and her bevy of cherries.
Ooh and aaah when the mushrooms and radishes whirl and twirl.

BOOK YOUR TICKETS 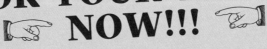 NOW!!!

HORRID
HENRY
RULES

HORRID HENRY'S COMPUTER

'No, no, no, no, no!' said Dad.

'No, no, no, no, no!' said Mum.

'The new computer is only for work,' said Dad. 'My work, Mum's work, and school work.'

'Not for playing silly games,' said Mum.

'But everyone plays games on their computer,' said Henry.

'Not in this house,' said Dad. He looked at the computer and frowned. 'Hmmn,' he said. 'How do you turn this thing off?'

'Like this,' said Horrid Henry. He pushed the 'off' button.

'Aha,' said Dad.

It was so unfair! Rude Ralph had *Intergalactic Robot Rebellion*. Dizzy Dave had *Snake Masters Revenge III*.

VIRTUAL CLASSROOM!

Kids! *No need to cry when it's time to leave school! Now you can have all the fun of school . . . at home! Take spelling tests! Practise fractions! Learn about the Tudors! It's fun fun fun with . . .*

VIRTUAL CLASSROOM!

Moody Margaret had *Zippy Zappers*. Horrid Henry had *Be a Spelling Champion, Whoopee for Numbers* and *Virtual Classroom*. Aside from Beefy Bert, who'd been given *Counting Made Easy* for Christmas, no one else had such awful software.

'What's the point of finally getting a computer if you can't play games?' said Horrid Henry.

'You can improve your spelling,' said Perfect Peter. 'And write essays. I've already written one for school tomorrow.'

'I don't want to improve my spelling!' screamed Henry. 'I want to play games!'

'I don't,' said Perfect Peter. 'Unless it's *Name that Vegetable* of course.'

'Quite right, Peter,' said Mum.

'You're the meanest parents in the world and I hate you,' shrieked Henry.

'You're the best parents in the world and I love you,' said Perfect Peter.

Horrid Henry had had enough. He leapt on Peter, snarling. He was the Loch Ness monster gobbling up a thrashing duck.

'OWWWWWW!'

squealed Peter.

'Go to your room, Henry!' shouted Dad. 'You're banned from the computer for a week.'

'We'll see about that,' muttered Horrid Henry, slamming his bedroom door.

Snore. Snore. Snore.

Horrid Henry sneaked past Mum and Dad's room and slipped downstairs.

There was the new computer. Henry sat down in front of it and looked longingly at the blank screen.

How could he get some games? He had 53p saved up. Not even enough for *Snake Masters Revenge I*, he thought miserably. Everyone he knew had fun on their computers. Everyone except him. He loved zapping aliens. He loved marshalling armies. He loved ruling the world. But no. His yucky parents would only let him have educational games. Ugh. When he was king anyone who wrote an educational game would be fed to the lions.

Horrid Henry sighed and switched on the computer. Maybe some games were hidden on the hard disk, he thought hopefully. Mum and Dad were scared of computers and wouldn't know how to look.

The word 'Password' flashed up on the screen.

I know a good password, thought Horrid Henry. Quickly he typed in 'Smelly Socks'.

smelly socks

Then Horrid Henry searched. And searched. And searched. But there were no hidden games. Just boring stuff like Mum's spreadsheets and Dad's reports.

Rats, thought Henry. He leaned back in the chair. Would it be fun to switch around some numbers in Mum's dreary spreadsheet? Or add a few words like 'yuck' and 'yah, boo, you're a ninny,' to Dad's stupid report?

Not really.

Wait, what was this? Perfect Peter's homework essay!

Let's see what he's written, thought Henry. Perfect Peter's essay appeared on the screen, titled, 'Why I love my teacher'.

Poor Peter, thought Henry. What a boring title. Let's see if I can improve it for him.

Tap tap tap.

Peter's essay was now called, 'Why I hate my teacher'. That's more like it, thought Henry. He read on.

'My teacher is the best. She's kind, she's fun, and she makes learning a joy. I am so lucky to be in Miss Lovely's class. Hip hip hooray for Miss Lovely.'

Oh dear. Worse and worse, thought Horrid Henry.

Tap tap tap.

'My teacher is the worst.' Still missing something, thought Henry.

Tap tap tap.

'My fat teacher is the worst.'

That's more like it, thought Henry. Now for the rest.

Tap tap tap tap tap.

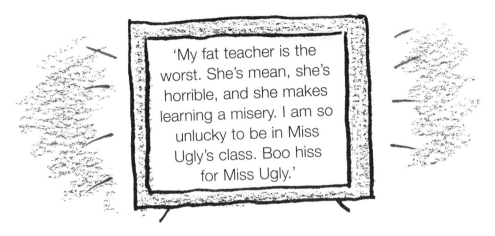

'My fat teacher is the worst. She's mean, she's horrible, and she makes learning a misery. I am so unlucky to be in Miss Ugly's class. Boo hiss for Miss Ugly.'

Much better.

Now that's what I call an essay, thought Horrid Henry. He pressed 'Save', then switched off the computer and tiptoed back to bed.

ARRRGGHHHH! AAAHHHH! NOOOOO!

Horrid Henry jumped out of bed. Mum was shrieking. Dad was shrieking. Peter was shrieking.

Honestly, couldn't anyone get any rest around here? He stomped down the stairs.

Everyone was gathered round the computer.

'Do something!' shouted Dad. 'I need that report now.'

'I'm trying!' shouted Mum. She pressed a few keys.

'It's jammed,' she said.

'My essay!' wailed Perfect Peter.

'My spreadsheet!' wailed Mum.

'My report!' wailed Dad.

'What's wrong?' said Henry.

'The computer's broken!' said Dad.

'How I hate these horrible machines,' said Mum.

'You've got to fix it,' said Dad. 'I've got to hand in my report this morning.'

'I can't,' said Mum. 'The computer won't let me in.'

'I don't understand,' said Dad. 'We've never needed a password before.'

Suddenly Horrid Henry realised what was wrong. He'd set a new password. No one could use the computer without it. Mum and Dad didn't know anything about passwords. All Horrid Henry had to do to fix the computer was to type in the password 'Smelly Socks.'

'I might be able to help, Dad,' said Horrid Henry.

'Really?' said Dad. He looked doubtful.

'Are you sure?' said Mum. She looked doubtful.

'I'll try,' said Horrid Henry. He sat down in front of the computer. 'Whoops, no I can't,' said Horrid Henry.

'Why not?' said Mum.

'I'm banned,' said Henry. 'Remember?'

'All right, you're unbanned,' said Dad, scowling. 'Just hurry up.'

'I have to be at school with my essay in ten minutes!' moaned Peter.

'And I have to get to work!' moaned Mum.

'I'll do my best,' said Horrid Henry slowly. 'But this is a very hard problem to solve.'

He tapped a few keys and frowned at the screen.

'Do you know what's wrong, Henry?' asked Dad.

'The hard disk is disconnected from the harder disk, and the hardest disk has slipped,' said Horrid Henry.

'Oh,' said Dad.

'Ahh,' said Mum.

'Huunh?' said Perfect Peter.

'You learn about that stuff in computer class next year,' said Horrid Henry. 'Now stand back, everyone, you're making me nervous.'

Mum, Dad, and Peter stepped back.

'You're our last hope, Henry,' said Mum.

'I will fix this on one condition,' said Henry.

'Anything,' said Dad.

'Anything,' said Mum.

'Deal,' said Horrid Henry, and typed in the password.

Whirr! Whirr! Spit!

Horrid Henry scooped up Mum's spreadsheet, Dad's report, and Perfect Peter's essay from the printer and handed them round.

'Thank you so much,' said Dad.

'Thank you so much,' said Mum.

Perfect Peter beamed at his beautifully printed essay, then put it carefully into his school bag. He'd never handed in a printed essay before. He couldn't wait to see what Miss Lovely said.

'Oh my goodness, Peter, what a smart looking essay you've written!' said Miss Lovely.

'It's all about you, Miss Lovely,' said Peter, beaming. 'Would you like to read it?'

'Of course,' said Miss Lovely. 'I'll read it to the class.'

She cleared her throat and began:

'Why I ha—' Miss Lovely stopped reading. Her face went pink.

'Peter!' she gasped. 'Go straight to the head! Now!'

'But – but – is it because my essay is so good?' squeaked Peter.

'NO!' said Miss Lovely.

'**Waaaaahhh!**' wailed Perfect Peter.

PEEEEOWWWW! BANG! RAT-A-TAT-TAT!

Another intergalactic robot bit the dust. Now, what shall I play next? thought Horrid Henry happily. *Snake Masters Revenge III*? *Zippy Zapper*? Best of all, Perfect Peter had been banned from the computer for a week,

after Miss Lovely had phoned Mum and Dad to tell them about Peter's rude essay. Peter blamed Henry. Henry blamed the computer.

TO THE MOODIEST MARGARET
Margaret, you old pants face
I've never seen such a nutcase
You are a stinky smelly toad
Won't I laugh when you explode

Ha ha ha to you too, smelly

Stinky

Pongy

Pooey

Whiffy

Odiferous

Odi – what?
Thats not a word.

Is too

Is not

HORRID HENRY
MEETS THE QUEEN

Perfect Peter bowed to himself in the mirror. 'Your Majesty,' he said, pretending to present a bouquet. 'Welcome to our school, your Majesty. My name is Peter, Your Majesty. Thank you, Your Majesty. Goodbye, Your Majesty.' Slowly Perfect Peter retreated backwards, bowing and smiling.

'Oh shut up,' snarled Horrid Henry. He glared at Peter. If Peter said 'Your Majesty' one more time, he would, he would – Horrid Henry wasn't sure what he'd do, but it would be horrible.

The Queen was coming to Henry's school! The real live Queen! The real live Queen, with her dogs and jewels and crowns and castles and beefeaters and knights and horses and ladies-in-waiting, was coming to see the Tudor wall they had built.

Yet for some reason Horrid Henry had not been asked to give the Queen a bouquet. Instead, the head, Mrs Oddbod, had chosen Peter.

Peter!

Why stupid smelly old ugly toad Peter? It was so unfair. Just because Peter had more stars than anyone in the 'Good as Gold' book, was that any reason to choose *him*? Henry should have been chosen. He would do a much better job than Peter. Besides, he wanted to ask the Queen how many TVs she had. Now he'd never get the chance.

'Your Majesty,' said Peter, bowing.

'Your Majesty,' mimicked Henry, curtseying.

Perfect Peter ignored him. He'd been ignoring Henry a lot ever since *he'd* been chosen to meet the queen. Come to think of it, everyone had been ignoring Henry.

'Isn't it thrilling?' said Mum for the millionth time.

'Isn't it fantastic?' said Dad for the billionth time.

'NO!' Henry had said. Who'd want to hand some rotten flowers to a stupid queen anyhow? Not Horrid Henry. And he certainly didn't want to have his picture in the paper, and everyone making a fuss.

'Bow, bouquet, answer her question, walk away,'

muttered Perfect Peter. Then he paused. 'Or is it bouquet, bow?'

Horrid Henry had had just about enough of Peter showing off.

'You're doing it all wrong,' said Henry.

'No I'm not,' said Peter.

'Yes you are,' said Henry. 'You're supposed to hold the bouquet up to her nose, so she can have a sniff before you give it to her.'

Perfect Peter paused.

'No I'm not,' said Peter.

Horrid Henry shook his head sadly. 'I think we'd better practice,' he said. 'Pretend I'm the Queen.' He picked up Peter's shiny silver crown, covered in fool's jewels, and put it on his head.

Perfect Peter beamed. He'd been begging Henry to practise with him all morning. 'Ask me a question the Queen would ask,' said Peter.

Horrid Henry considered.

'Why are you so smelly, little boy?' said the Queen, holding her nose.

'The Queen wouldn't ask *that*!' gasped Perfect Peter.

'Yes she would,' said Henry.

'Wouldn't.'

'Would.'

'And I'm not smelly!'

Horrid Henry waved his hand in front of his face.

'Poo!' said the Queen. 'Take this smelly boy to the Tower.'

'Stop it, Henry,' said Peter. 'Ask me a real question, like my name or what year I'm in.'

'Why are you so ugly?' said the Queen.

'MUM!' wailed Peter. 'Henry called me ugly. And smelly.'

'Don't be horrid, Henry!' shouted Mum.

'Do you want me to practise with you or don't you?' hissed Henry.

'Practise,' sniffed Peter.

'Well, go on then,' said Henry.

Perfect Peter walked up to Henry and bowed.

'Wrong!' said Henry. 'You don't bow to the Queen, you curtsey.'

'Curtsey?' said Peter. Mrs Oddbod hadn't said anything about curtseying. 'But I'm a boy.'

'The law was changed,' said Henry. 'Everyone curtseys now.'

Peter hesitated.

'Are you sure?' asked Peter.

'Yes,' said Henry. 'And when you meet the Queen, you put your thumb on your nose and wriggle your fingers. Like this.'

Horrid Henry cocked a snook.

Perfect Peter gasped. Mrs Oddbod hadn't said anything about thumbs on noses.

'But that's . . . rude,' said Perfect Peter.

'Not to the Queen,' said Horrid Henry. 'You can't just say 'hi' to the Queen like she's a person. She's the Queen. There are special rules. If you get it wrong she can chop off your head.'

Chop off his head! Mrs Oddbod hadn't said anything about chopping off heads.

'That's not true,' said Peter.

'Yes it is,' said Henry.

'Isn't!'

Horrid Henry sighed. 'If you get it wrong, you'll be locked up in the Tower,' he said. 'It's high treason to greet the Queen the wrong way. *Everyone* knows that.'

Perfect Peter paused. Mrs Oddbod hadn't said anything about being locked up in the Tower.

'I don't believe you, Henry,' said Peter.

Henry shrugged.

'Okay. Just don't blame me when you get your head chopped off.'

Come to think of it, thought Peter, there *was* a lot of head-chopping when people met kings and queens. But surely that was just in the olden days . . .

'MUM!' screamed Peter.

Mum ran into the room.

'Henry said I had to curtsey to the Queen,' wailed Peter. 'And that I'd get my head chopped off if I got it wrong.'

Mum glared at Henry.

'How *could* you be so horrid, Henry?' said Mum. 'Go to your room!'

'Fine!' screeched Horrid Henry.

'I'll practise with you, Peter,' said Mum.

'Bow, bouquet, answer her question, walk away,' said Peter, beaming.

The great day arrived. The entire school lined up in the playground, waiting for the Queen. Perfect Peter, dressed in his best party clothes, stood with Mrs Oddbod by the gate.

A large black car pulled up in front of the school.

'There she is!' shrieked the children.

Horrid Henry was furious. Miss Battle-Axe had made him stand in the very last row, as far away from the Queen as he could be. How on earth could he find out if she had 300 TVs standing way back here? Anyone would think Miss Battle-Axe wanted to keep him away from the Queen on purpose, thought Henry, scowling.

Perfect Peter waited, clutching an enormous bouquet of flowers. His big moment was here.

'Bow, bouquet, answer her question, walk away. Bow, bouquet, answer her question, walk away,' mumbled Peter.

'Don't worry, Peter, you'll be perfect,' whispered Mrs Oddbod, urging him forward.

Horrid Henry pushed and shoved to get a closer view. Yes, there was his stupid brother, looking like a worm.

Perfect Peter walked slowly towards the Queen.

'Bow, bouquet, answer her question, walk away,' he mumbled. Suddenly that didn't sound right.

Was it bow, bouquet? Or bouquet, bow?

The Queen looked down at Peter.

Peter looked up at the Queen.

'Your Majesty,' he said.

Now what was he supposed to do next?

Peter's heart began to pound. His mind was blank.

Peter bowed. The bouquet smacked him in the face.

'Oww!' yelped Peter.

What had he practised? Ah yes, now he remembered!

Peter curtseyed. Then he cocked a snook.

Mrs Oddbod gasped.

Oh no, what had he done wrong?

Aaarrgh, the bouquet! It was still in his hand.

Quickly Peter thrust it at the Queen.

Smack!

The flowers hit her in the face.

'How lovely,' said the Queen.

'Waaaa!' wailed Peter. 'Don't chop off my head!'

There was a very long silence. Henry saw his chance.

'How many TVs have you got?' shouted Horrid Henry.

The Queen did not seem to have heard.

'Come along everyone, to the display of Tudor daub-making,' said Mrs Oddbod. She looked a little pale.

'I said,' shouted Henry, 'how many—' A long, bony arm yanked him away.

'Be quiet, Henry,' hissed Miss Battle-Axe. 'Go to the back playground like we practised. I don't want to hear another word out of you.'

Horrid Henry trudged off to the vat of daub with Miss Battle-Axe's beady eyes watching his every step. It was so unfair!

When everyone was in their assigned place, Mrs Oddbod spoke. 'Your Majesty, mums and dads, boys and girls, the Tudors used mud and straw to make daub for their walls. Miss Battle-Axe's class will now show you how.' She nodded to the children standing in the vat. The school recorder band played *Greensleeves*.

Henry's class began to stomp in the vat of mud and straw.

'How lovely,' said the Queen.

Horrid Henry stomped where he'd been placed between Jazzy Jim and Aerobic Al. There was a whole vat of stomping children blocking him from the Queen, who was seated in the front row between Miss Battle-Axe and Mrs Oddbod. If only he could get closer to the Queen. Then he could find out about those TVs!

Henry noticed a tiny space between Brainy Brian and Gorgeous Gurinder.

Henry stomped his way through it.

'Hey!' said Brian.

'Oww!' said Gurinder. 'That was my foot!'

Henry ignored them.

Stomp Stomp Stomp

Henry pounded past Greedy Graham and Weepy William.

'Oy!' said Graham. 'Stop pushing.'

'Waaaaaaa!' wept Weepy William.

Halfway to the front!

Henry pushed past Anxious Andrew and Clever Clare.

'Hellllppp!' squeaked Andrew, falling over.

'Watch out, Henry,' snapped Clare.

Almost there! Just Moody Margaret and Jolly Josh stood in his way.

Margaret stomped.

Josh stomped.

Henry trampled through the daub till he stood right behind Margaret.

SQUISH. SQUASH. SQUISH. SQUASH.

'Stop stomping on my bit,' hissed Moody Margaret.

'Stop stomping on *my* bit,' said Horrid Henry.

270

'I was here first,' said Margaret.

'No you weren't,' said Henry. 'Now get out of my way.'

'Make me,' said Moody Margaret.

Henry stomped harder.

SQUELCH! SQUELCH! SQUELCH!

Margaret stomped harder.

STOMP! STOMP! STOMP!

Rude Ralph pushed forward. So did Dizzy Dave.

STOMP! STOMP! STOMP!

Sour Susan pushed forward. So did Kung-Fu Kate.

STOMP! STOMP! STOMP! STOMP! STOMP!

A tidal wave of mud and straw flew out of the vat.

SPLAT!

Miss Battle-Axe was covered.

SPLAT!

Mrs Oddbod was covered.

SPLAT!

The Queen was covered.
'Oops,' said Horrid Henry.
Mrs Oddbod fainted.
'How lovely,' mumbled the Queen.

Buckingham Palace

Dear Mrs Oddbod

The Queen has commanded me to thank you for inviting her to your school to see your lovely display of Tudor daub-making. Enclosed please find a cleaning bill.

Yours sincerely

Hrothgar Frothington

Sir Hrothgar Frothington
Private Secretary to the Queen

CROWN CLEANERS
By Appointment to Her Majesty the Queen

For scrubbing and polishing orb and sceptre	£641.99
For scrubbing and polishing crown	£8,740.08
For dry-cleaning and repairing ermine robes	£12,672.39
Grand total	£22,053.96

PAYABLE NEXT TUESDAY BY ORDER OF
HER MAJESTY
OR ELSE

PERFECT PETER'S REVENGE

Perfect Peter had had enough. Why oh why did he always fall for Henry's tricks?

Every time it happened he swore Henry would never ever trick him again. And every time he fell for it. How *could* he have believed that there were fairies at the bottom of the garden? Or that there was such a thing as a Fangmangler? But the time machine was the worst. The very very worst. Everyone had teased him. Even Goody-Goody Gordon asked him if he'd seen any spaceships recently.

Well, never again. His mean, horrible brother had tricked him for the very last time.

I'll get my revenge, thought Perfect Peter, pasting the last of his animal stamps into his album. I'll make Henry sorry for being so mean to me.

But what horrid mean nasty thing could he do? Peter had never tried to be revenged on anyone.

He asked Tidy Ted.

'Mess up his room,' said Ted.

But Henry's room was already a mess.

He asked Spotless Sam.

'Put a spaghetti stain on his shirt,' said Sam.

But Henry's shirts were already stained.

Peter picked up a copy of his favourite magazine *Best Boy*. Maybe it would have some handy hints on the perfect revenge. He searched the table of contents:

☺ BEST BOY ☺

❀ Is YOUR bedroom as tidy as it could be?

❀ Ten top tips for pleasing your parents

❀ How to polish your trophies

❀ Why making your bed is good for you

❀ Readers tell us about their **FAVOURITE** chores!

Reluctantly, Peter closed *Best Boy* magazine. Somehow he didn't think he'd find the answer inside. He was on his own.

I'll tell Mum that Henry eats sweets in his bedroom, thought Peter. Then Henry would get into trouble. Big big trouble.

But Henry got into trouble all the time. That wouldn't be anything special.

I know, thought Peter, I'll hide Mr Kill. Henry would never admit it, but he couldn't sleep without Mr Kill. But so what if Henry couldn't sleep? He'd just come and jump on Peter's head or sneak downstairs and watch scary movies. I have to think of something really, really horrid, thought Peter. It was hard for Peter to think horrid thoughts, but Peter was determined to try.

He would call Henry a horrid name, like Ugly Toad or Poo Poo face. *That* would show him.

But if I did Henry would hit me, thought Peter. Wait, he could tell everyone at school that Henry wore nappies. Henry the big nappy. Henry the big smelly nappy. Henry nappy face. Henry poopy pants. Peter smiled happily. That would be a perfect revenge.

Then he stopped smiling. Sadly, no one at school would believe that Henry still wore nappies. Worse, they might think that Peter still did! Eeeek.

I've got it, thought Peter, I'll put a muddy twig in Henry's bed. Peter had read a great story about a younger brother who'd done just that to a mean older one. That would serve Henry right.

But was a muddy twig enough revenge for all of Henry's crimes against him?

No it was not.

I give up, thought Peter, sighing. It was hopeless. He just couldn't think of anything horrid enough.

Peter sat down on his beautifully made bed and opened *Best Boy* magazine.

TELL MUM HOW MUCH YOU LOVE HER!

shrieked the headline.

And then a dreadful thought tiptoed into his head. It was so dreadful, and so horrid, that Perfect Peter could not believe that he had thought it.

'No,' he gasped. 'I couldn't.' That was too evil.

But . . . but . . . wasn't that exactly what he wanted? A horrid revenge on a horrid brother?

'Don't do it!' begged his angel.

'Do it!' urged his devil, thrilled to get the chance to speak. 'Go on, Peter! Henry deserves it.'

YES! thought Peter. He would do it. He would be revenged!

Perfect Peter sat down at the computer.

Tap tap tap.

Dear Margaret,
I love you. Will
you marry me?

Peter printed out the note and carefully scrawled:

Henry

There! thought Peter proudly. That looks just like Henry's writing. He folded the note, then sneaked into the garden, climbed over the wall, and left it on the table inside Moody Margaret's Secret Club tent.

'Of course Henry loves me,' said Moody Margaret, preening. 'He can't help it. Everyone loves me because I'm so lovable.'

'No you're not,' said Sour Susan. 'You're moody. And you're mean.'

'Am not!'

'Are too!'

'Am not. You're just jealous 'cause no one would *ever* want to marry you,' snapped Margaret.

'I am not jealous. Anyway, Henry likes *me* the best,' said Susan, waving a folded piece of paper.

'Says who?'

'Says Henry.'

Margaret snatched the paper from Susan's hand and read:

to the Beautiful Susan

Oh Susan,
No one is as pretty as you,
You always smell lovely
Just like shampoo.

Henry

Margaret sniffed. 'Just like dog poo, you mean.'

'I do not,' shrieked Susan.

'Is this your idea of a joke?' snorted Moody Margaret, crumpling the poem.

Sour Susan was outraged.

'No. It was waiting for me on the clubhouse table.

You're just jealous because Henry didn't write *you* a poem.'

'Huh,' said Margaret. Well, she'd show Henry. No one made a fool of her.

Margaret snatched up a pen and scribbled a reply to Henry's note.

'Take this to Henry and report straight back,' she ordered. 'I'll wait here for Linda and Gurinder.'

'Take it yourself,' said Susan sourly. Why oh why was she friends with such a mean, moody jealous grump?

Horrid Henry was inside the Purple Hand Fort plotting death to the Secret Club and scoffing biscuits when an enemy agent peered through the entrance.

'Guard!' shrieked Henry.

But that miserable worm toad was nowhere to be found.

Henry reminded himself to sack Peter immediately.

'Halt! Who goes there?'

'I have an important message,' said the Enemy.

'Make it snappy,' said Henry. 'I'm busy.'

Susan crept beneath the branches.

'Do you really like my shampoo, Henry?' she asked.

Henry stared at Susan. She had a sick smile on her face, as if her stomach hurt.

'Huh?' said Henry.

'You know, my *shampoo*,' said Susan, simpering.

Had Susan finally gone mad?

'*That's* your message?' said Horrid Henry.

'No,' said Susan, scowling. She tossed a scrunched-up piece of paper at Henry and marched off.

Henry opened the note:

I wouldn't marry you if you were the last creature on earth and that includes slimy toads and rattlesnakes. So there.

Margaret

Henry choked on his biscuit. Marry Margaret?! He'd rather walk around town carrying a Walkie-Talkie-Burpy-Slurpy-Teasy-Weasy Doll. He'd rather learn long division. He'd rather trade all his computer games for a Princess Pamper Parlour. He'd rather . . . he'd rather . . . he'd rather marry Miss Battle-Axe than marry Margaret!

What on earth had given Margaret the crazy, horrible, revolting idea he wanted to marry *her*?

He always knew Margaret was nuts. Now he had proof. Well well well, thought Horrid Henry gleefully. Wouldn't he tease her! Margaret would never live this down.

Henry leapt over the wall and burst into the Secret Club Tent.

'Margaret, you old pants face, I wouldn't marry you if –'

'Henry loves Margaret! Henry loves Margaret!' chanted Gorgeous Gurinder.

'Henry loves Margaret! Henry loves Margaret!' chanted Lazy Linda, making horrible kissing sounds.

Henry tried to speak. He opened his mouth. Then he closed it.

'No I don't,' gasped Horrid Henry.

'Oh yeah?' said Gurinder.

'Yeah,' said Henry.

'Then why'd you send her a note saying you did?'

'I didn't!' howled Henry.

'And you sent Susan a poem!' said Linda.

'I DID NOT!' howled Henry even louder. What on earth was going on? He took a step backwards.

The Secret Club members advanced on him, shrieking, 'Henry loves Margaret, Henry loves Margaret.'

Time, thought Horrid Henry, to beat a strategic retreat. He dashed back to his fort, the terrible words 'Henry loves Margaret' burning his ears.

'PETER!' bellowed Horrid Henry. 'Come here this minute!'

Perfect Peter crept out of the house to the fort. Henry had found out about the note and the poem. He was dead.

Goodbye, cruel world, thought Peter.

'Did you see anyone going into the Secret Club carrying a note?' demanded Henry, glaring.

Perfect Peter's heart began to beat again.

'No,' said Peter. That wasn't a lie because he hadn't seen himself.

'I want you to stand guard by the wall, and report anyone suspicious to me at once,' said Henry.

'Why?' said Peter innocently.

'None of your business, worm,' snapped Henry. 'Just do as you're told.'

'Yes, Lord High Excellent Majesty of the Purple Hand,' said Perfect Peter. What a lucky escape!

Henry sat on his Purple Hand throne and considered. Who was this foul fiend? Who was this evil genius? Who was spreading these foul rumours? He had to find out, then strike back hard before the snake struck again.

But who'd want to be his enemy? He was such a nice, kind, friendly boy.

True, Rude Ralph wasn't very happy when Henry called him Ralphie Walfie.

Tough Toby wasn't too pleased when Henry debagged him during playtime.

And for some reason, Brainy Brian didn't see the joke when Henry scribbled all over his book report.

Vain Violet said she'd pay Henry back for pulling her pigtails.

And just the other day Fiery Fiona said Henry would be sorry he'd laughed during her speech in assembly.

Even Kind Kasim warned Henry to stop being so horrid or he'd teach him a lesson he wouldn't forget.

But maybe Margaret was behind the whole plot. He had stinkbombed her Secret Club, after all.

Hmmn. The list of suspects was rather long.

It had to be Ralph. Ralph loved playing practical jokes.

Well, it's not funny, Ralph, thought Horrid Henry. Let's see how *you* like it. Perhaps a little poem to Miss Battle-Axe . . .

Horrid Henry grabbed a piece of paper and began to scribble:

> Oh Boudicca dear,
> Whenever you're near,
> I just want to cheer,
> Oh big old teacher
> Your carrot nose is your best feature
> You are so sweet
> I would like to kiss your feet
> What a treat
> Even though they smell of meat
> Dear Miss Battle-Axe
> Clear out your earwax
> So you can hear me say...
> No need to frown
> But your pants are falling down!

Ha ha ha ha ha, thought Henry. He'd sign the poem 'Ralph', get to school early and pin the poem on the door of the Girls' Toilet. Ralph would get into big big trouble.

But wait.

What if Ralph *wasn't* responsible? Could it be Toby after all? Or Margaret? There was only one thing to do.

Henry copied his poem seven times, signing each copy with a different name. He would post them all over school tomorrow. One of them was sure to be guilty.

Henry sneaked into school, then quickly pinned up his poems on every noticeboard. That done, he swaggered onto the playground. Revenge is sweet, thought Horrid Henry.

There was a crowd gathered outside the boys' toilets.

'What's going on?' shrieked Horrid Henry, pushing

and shoving his way through the crowd.

'Henry loves Margaret,' chanted Tough Toby.

'Henry loves Margaret,' chanted Rude Ralph.

Uh oh.

Henry glanced at the toilet door. There was a note taped on it.

Dear Margaret
I love you.
Will you marry me?
Henry

Henry's blood froze. He ripped the note off the door.

'Margaret wrote it to herself,' blustered Horrid Henry.

'Didn't!' said Margaret.

'Did!' said Henry.

'Besides, you love *me*!' shrieked Susan.

'No I don't!' shrieked Henry.

'That's 'cause you love me!' said Margaret.

'I hate you!' shouted Henry.

'I hate you more!' said Margaret.

'I hate *you* more,' said Henry.

'You started it,' said Margaret.

'Didn't.'

'Did! You asked me to marry you.'

'NO WAY!' shrieked Henry.

'And you sent me a poem!' said Susan.

'No I didn't!' howled Henry.

'Well, if you didn't then who did?' said Margaret.

Silence.

'Henry,' came a little voice, 'can we play pirates after school today?'

Horrid Henry thought an incredible thought.

Moody Margaret thought an incredible thought.

Sour Susan thought an incredible thought.

Three pairs of eyes stared at Perfect Peter.

'Wha . . . what?' said Peter.

Uh oh.

'HELP!' shrieked Perfect Peter. He turned and ran.

AAAARRRRGHHHHHH!

shrieked Horrid Henry, chasing after him. 'You're dead meat, worm!'

Miss Battle-Axe marched onto the playground. She was clutching a sheaf of papers in her hand.

'Margaret! Brian! Ralph! Toby! Violet! Kasim! Fiona! What is the meaning of these poems? Straight to the head – now!'

Perfect Peter crashed into her.

Miss Battle-Axe toppled backwards into the bin.

'And you too, Peter,' gasped Miss Battle-Axe.

wailed Perfect Peter. From now on, he'd definitely be sticking to good deeds. Whoever said revenge was sweet didn't have a horrid brother like Henry.

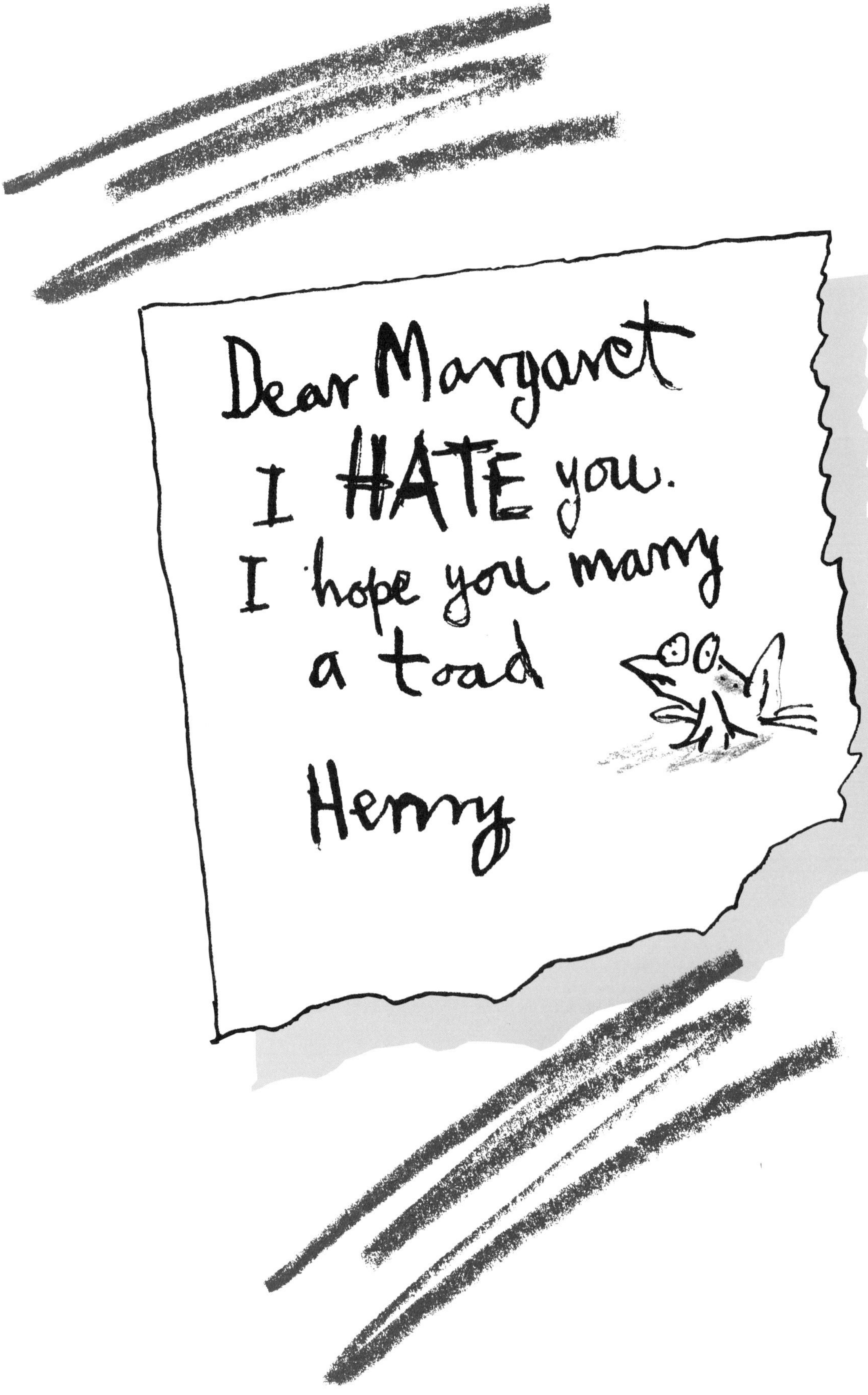
Dear Margaret
I HATE you.
I hope you marry
a toad
Henry

A toad would rather get
squished in the road
than marry you,
So ha ha ha.
Margaret.

HORRID HENRY
AND THE
FOOTBALL FIEND

'A . . . ND with 15 seconds to go it's Hot-Foot Henry racing across the pitch! Rooney tries a slide tackle but Henry's too quick! Just look at that step-over! Oh no, he can't score from that distance, it's crazy, it's impossible, oh my goodness, he cornered the ball, it's IN!!!! It's IN! Another *spectacular* goal! Another spectacular win! And it's all thanks to Hot-Foot Henry, the greatest footballer who's ever lived!'

'Goal! Goal! Goal!' roared the crowd. Hot-Foot Henry had won the match! His teammates carried him through the fans, cheering and chanting, 'Hen-ry! Hen-ry! Hen-ry!'

'HENRY!'

Horrid Henry looked up to see Miss Battle-Axe leaning over his table and glaring at him with her red eyes.

'What did I just say?'

'Henry,' said Horrid Henry.

Miss Battle-Axe scowled.

'I'm watching you, Henry,' she snapped. 'Now class, please pay attention, we need to discuss—'

'Waaaaa!' wailed Weepy William.

'Susan, stop pulling my hair!' squealed Vain Violet.

'Miss!' shouted Inky Ian, 'Ralph's snatched my pen!'

'Didn't!' shouted Rude Ralph.

'Did!' shouted Inky Ian.

'Class! Be quiet!' bellowed Miss Battle-Axe.

'Waaaaa!' wailed Weepy William.

'Owwww!' squealed Vain Violet.

'Give it back!' shouted Inky Ian.

'Fine,' said Miss Battle-Axe, 'we won't talk about football.'

William stopped wailing.

Violet stopped squealing.

Ian stopped shouting.

Henry stopped daydreaming.

Everyone in the class stared at Miss Battle-Axe. Miss Battle-Axe wanted to talk about . . . football? Was this an alien Miss Battle-Axe?

'As you all know, our local team, Ashton Athletic, has reached the sixth round of the FA Cup,' said Miss Battle-Axe.

'YEY!' shrieked the class.

'And I'm sure you all know what happened last night . . .'

Last night! Henry could still hear the announcer's glorious words as he and Peter had gathered round the radio as the draw for round six was announced.

'Number 16, Ashton Athletic, will be playing . . .' there was a long pause as the announcer drew another ball from the hat . . . 'number 7, Manchester United.'

'Go Ashton!' shrieked Horrid Henry.

'As I was saying, before I was so rudely interrupted—' Miss Battle-Axe glared at Horrid Henry, 'Ashton are playing Manchester United in a few weeks. Every local primary school has been given a pair of tickets. And thanks to my good luck in the teacher's draw, the lucky winner will come from our class.'

'Me!' screamed Horrid Henry.

'Me!' screamed Moody Margaret.

'Me!' screamed Tough Toby, Aerobic Al, Fiery Fiona and Brainy Brian.

'No one who shouts out will be getting anything,' said Miss Battle-Axe. 'Our class will be playing a football match at lunchtime. The player of the match will win the tickets. I'm the referee and my decision will be final.'

Horrid Henry was so stunned that for a moment he could scarcely breathe. FA Cup tickets! FA Cup tickets to see his local team Ashton play against Man U! Those tickets were like gold dust. Henry had begged and pleaded with Mum and Dad to get tickets, but naturally they were all sold out by the time Henry's mean, horrible, lazy parents managed to heave their stupid bones to the phone. And now here was another chance to go to the match of the century!

Ashton Athletic had never got so far in the Cup. Sure, they'd knocked out the Tooting Tigers (chant: Toot Toot! Grrr!) the Pynchley Pythons and the Cheam Champions but—Manchester United! Henry had to go to the game. He just had to. And all he had to do was be man of the match.

There was just one problem. Unfortunately, the best footballer in the class wasn't Horrid Henry. Or Aerobic Al. Or Beefy Bert.

The best footballer in the class was Moody Margaret.

The second best player in the class was Moody Margaret. The third best player in the class was Moody Margaret. It was so unfair! Why should Margaret of all people be so fantastic at football?

Horrid Henry was brilliant at shirt pulling. Horrid Henry was superb at screaming 'Offside!' (whatever that meant). No one could howl 'Come on, ref!' louder.

And at toe-treading, elbowing, barging, pushing, shoving and tripping, Horrid Henry had no equal. The only thing Horrid Henry wasn't good at was playing football.

But never mind. Today would be different. Today he would dig deep inside and find the power to be Hot-Foot Henry—for real. Today no one would stop him. FA Cup match here I come, thought Horrid Henry gleefully.

Lunchtime!

Horrid Henry's class dashed to the back play-ground, where the pitch was set up. Two jumpers either end marked the goals. A few parents gathered on the sidelines.

Miss Battle-Axe split the class into two teams: Aerobic Al was captain of Henry's team, Moody Margaret was captain of the other.

There she stood in midfield, having nabbed a striker position, smirking confidently. Horrid Henry glared at her from the depths of the outfield.

'Na na ne nah nah, I'm sure to be man of the match,' trilled Moody Margaret, sticking out her tongue at him. 'And you-ooo won't.'

'Shut up, Margaret,' said Henry. When he was king,

anyone named Margaret would be boiled in oil and fed to the crows.

'Will you take me to the match, Margaret?' said Susan. 'After all, *I'm* your best friend.'

Moody Margaret scowled. 'Since when?'

'Since always!' wailed Susan.

'Huh!' said Margaret. 'We'll just have to see how nice you are to me, won't we?'

'Take me,' begged Brainy Brian. 'Remember how I helped you with those fractions?'

'And called me stupid,' said Margaret.

'Didn't,' said Brian.

'Did,' said Margaret.

Horrid Henry eyed his classmates. Everyone looking straight ahead, everyone determined to be man of the match. Well, wouldn't they be in for a shock when Horrid Henry waltzed off with those tickets!

'Go Margaret!' screeched Moody Margaret's mum.

'Go Al!' screeched Aerobic Al's dad.

'Everyone ready?' said Miss Battle-Axe. 'Bert! Which team are you on?'

'I dunno,' said Beefy Bert.

Miss Battle-Axe blew her whistle.

Henry stood disconsolately on the left wing, running back and forth as the play passed him by. How could he ever be man of the match stuck out here? Well, no way was he staying in this stupid spot a moment longer.

Horrid Henry abandoned his position and chased after the ball. All the other defenders followed him.

Moody Margaret had the ball. Horrid Henry ran up behind her. He glanced at Miss Battle-Axe. She was busy chatting to Mrs Oddbod. Horrid Henry went for a two foot slide tackle and tripped her.

'Foul!' screeched Margaret. 'He hacked my leg!'

'Liar!' screeched Henry. 'I just went for the ball!'

'Cheater!' screamed Moody Margaret's mum.

'Play on,' ordered Miss Battle-Axe.

Yes! thought Horrid Henry triumphantly. After all, what did blind old Miss Battle-Axe know about the rules of football? Nothing. This was his golden chance to score.

Now Jazzy Jim had the ball.

Horrid Henry trod on his toes, elbowed him, and grabbed the ball.

'Hey, we're on the same team!' yelped Jim.

Horrid Henry kept dribbling.

'Pass! Pass!' screamed Al. 'Man on!'

Henry ignored him. Pass the ball? Was Al mad? For once Henry had the ball and he was keeping it.

Then suddenly Moody Margaret appeared from behind, barged him, dribbled the ball past Henry's team and kicked it straight past Weepy William into goal. Moody Margaret's team cheered.

Weepy William burst into tears.
'Waaaaaa,' wailed Weepy William.
'Idiot!' screamed Aerobic Al's dad.
'She cheated!' shrieked Henry. 'She fouled me!'
'Didn't,' said Margaret.

'How dare you call my daughter a cheater?' screamed Margaret's mum.

Miss Battle-Axe blew her whistle.

'Goal to Margaret's team. The score is one-nil.'

Horrid Henry gritted his teeth. He would score a goal if he had to trample on every player to do so.

Unfortunately, everyone else seemed to have the same idea.

'Ralph pushed me!' shrieked Aerobic Al.

'Didn't!' lied Rude Ralph. 'It was just a barge.'

'He used his hands, I saw him!' howled Al's father. 'Send him off.'

'I'll send *you* off if you don't behave,' snapped Miss Battle-Axe, looking up and blowing her whistle.

'It was kept in!' protested Henry.

'No way!' shouted Margaret. 'It went past the line!'

'That was ball to hand!' yelled Kind Kasim.

'No way!' screamed Aerobic Al. 'I just went for the ball.'

'Liar!'

'Liar!'

'Free kick to Margaret's team,' said Miss Battle-Axe.

'Ouch!' screamed Soraya, as Brian stepped on her toes, grabbed the ball, and headed it into goal past Kasim.

'Hurray!' cheered Al's team.

'Foul!' screamed Margaret's team.

'Score is one all,' said Miss Battle-Axe. 'Five more minutes to go.'

AAARRRGGHH!

thought Horrid Henry. I've got to score a goal to have a chance to be man of the match. I've just got to. But how, how?

Henry glanced at Miss Battle-Axe. She appeared to be rummaging in her handbag. Henry saw his chance. He stuck out his foot as Margaret hurtled past.

CRASH!

Margaret tumbled.

Henry seized the ball.

'Henry hacked my leg!' shrieked Margaret.

'Did not!' shrieked Henry. 'I just went for the ball.'

'REF!' screamed Margaret.

'He cheated!' screamed Margaret's mum. 'Are you blind, ref?'

Miss Battle-Axe glared.

'My eyesight is perfect, thank you,' she snapped.

Tee hee, chortled Horrid Henry.

Henry trod on Brian's toes, elbowed him, then grabbed the ball. Then Dave elbowed Henry, Ralph trod on Dave's toes, and Susan seized the ball and kicked it high overhead.

Henry looked up. The ball was high, high up. He'd never reach it, not unless, unless— Henry glanced at

Miss Battle-Axe. She was watching a traffic warden patrolling outside the school gate. Henry leapt into the air and whacked the ball with his hand.

THWACK!

The ball hurled across the goal.

'Goal!' screamed Henry.

'He used his hands!' protested Margaret.

'No way!' shouted Henry. 'It was the hand of God!'

'Hen-ry! Hen-ry! Hen-ry!' cheered his team.

'Unfair!' howled Margaret's team.

Miss Battle-Axe blew her whistle.

'Time!' she bellowed. 'Al's team wins 2–1.'

'Yes!' shrieked Horrid Henry, punching the air. He'd scored the winning goal! He'd be man of the match! Ashton Athletic versus Man U here I come!

Horrid Henry's class limped through the door and sat down. Horrid Henry sat at the front, beaming. Miss Battle-Axe had to award him the tickets after his brilliant performance and spectacular, game-winning goal. The question was, who *deserved* to be his guest?

No one.

I know, thought Horrid Henry, I'll sell my other ticket. Bet I get a million pounds for it. No, a billion pounds. Then I'll buy my own team, and play striker any time I want to. Horrid Henry smiled happily.

Miss Battle-Axe glared at her class.

'That was absolutely disgraceful,' she said. 'Cheating! Moving the goals! Shirt tugging!' she glared at Graham. 'Barging!

She glowered at Ralph. 'Pushing and shoving! Bad sportsmanship!' Her eyes swept over the class.

Horrid Henry sank lower in his seat.

Oops.

'And don't get me started about offside,' she snapped.

Horrid Henry sank even lower.

'There was only one person who deserves to be

player of the match,' she continued. 'One person who observed the rules of the beautiful game. One person who has nothing to be ashamed of today.'

Horrid Henry's heart leapt. *He* certainly had nothing to be ashamed of.

'. . . One person who can truly be proud of their performance . . .'

Horrid Henry beamed with pride.

'And that person is—'

'Me! screamed Moody Margaret.

'Me!' screamed Aerobic Al.

'Me! screamed Horrid Henry.

'—the referee,' said Miss Battle-Axe.

What?

Miss Battle-Axe . . . man of the match?

Miss Battle-Axe . . . a football fiend?

'IT'S NOT FAIR!'
screamed the class.

'IT'S NOT FAIR!'
screamed Horrid Henry.

HORRID HENRY'S SICK DAY

Cough! Cough! Sneeze! Sneeze!

'Are you all right, Peter?' asked Mum.

Peter coughed, choked, and spluttered.

'I'm OK,' he gasped.

'Are you sure?' said Dad. 'You don't look very well.'

'It's nothing,' said Perfect Peter, coughing.

Mum felt Peter's sweaty brow.

'You've got a temperature,' said Mum. 'I think you'd better stay home from school today.'

'But I don't want to miss school,' said Peter.

'Go back to bed,' said Mum.

'But I want to go to school,' wailed Peter. 'I'm sure I'll be—' Peter's pale, sweaty face turned green. He dashed up the stairs to the loo. Mum ran after him.

Bleeeeeeecchhhh

The horrible sound of vomiting filled the house.

Horrid Henry stopped eating his toast. Peter, stay at home? Peter, miss school? Peter, laze about watching TV while he, Henry, had to suffer a long hard day with Miss Battle-Axe?

No way! He was sick, too. Hadn't he coughed twice this morning? And he had definitely sneezed last night. Now that he thought about it, he could feel those flu germs invading. Yup, there they were, marching down his throat.

Stomp stomp stomp marched the germs. Mercy! shrieked his throat. Ha ha ha gloated the germs.

Horrid Henry thought about those spelling words he hadn't learnt. The map he hadn't finished colouring. The book report he hadn't done.

Oww. His throat hurt.

Oooh. His tummy hurt.

Eeek. His head hurt.

Yippee! He was sick!

So what would it be?

Maths or Mutant Max?

Reading or relaxing?

Commas or comics?

Tests or TV?

Hmmm, thought Horrid Henry. Hard choice.

COUGH. COUGH.

Dad continued reading the paper.

COUGH! COUGH! COUGH! COUGH! COUGH!

'Are you all right, Henry?' asked Dad, without looking up.

'No!' gasped Henry. 'I'm sick, too. I can't go to school.'

Slowly Dad put down his newspaper.

'You don't look ill, Henry,' said Dad.

'But I am,' whimpered Horrid Henry. He clutched his throat. 'My throat really hurts,' he moaned. Then he added a few coughs, just in case.

'I feel weak,' he groaned. 'Everything aches.'

Dad sighed.

'All right, you can stay home,' he said.

Yes! thought Horrid Henry. He was amazed. It usually took much more moaning and groaning before his mean, horrible parents decided he was sick enough to miss a day of school.

'But no playing on the computer,' said Dad. 'If you're sick, you have to lie down.'

Horrid Henry was outraged.

'But it makes me feel better to play on the computer,' he protested.

'If you're well enough to play on the computer, you're well enough to go to school,' said Dad.

Rats.

Oh well, thought Horrid Henry. He'd get his duvet, lie on the sofa and watch loads of TV instead. Then Mum would bring him cold drinks, lunch on a tray, maybe even ice cream. It was always such a waste when you were too sick to enjoy being sick, thought Horrid Henry happily.

He could hear Mum and Dad arguing upstairs.

'I need to go to work,' said Mum.

'I need to go to work,' said Dad.

'I stayed home last time,' said Mum.

'No you didn't, I did,' said Dad.

'Are you sure?' said Mum.

'Yes,' said Dad.

'Are you sure you're sure?' said Mum.

Horrid Henry could hardly believe his ears. Imagine arguing over who got to stay home! When he was grown-up he was going to stay home full time, testing computer games for a million pounds a week.

He bounced into the sitting room. Then he stopped bouncing. A horrible, ugly, snotty creature was stretched out under a duvet in the comfy black chair. Horrid Henry glanced at the TV. A dreadful assortment of wobbling creatures were dancing and prancing.

TRA LA LA LA LA,
WE LIVE AT NELLIE'S
WE'VE ALL GOT BIG BELLIES
WE EAT PURPLE JELLIES
AT NELLIE'S NURSERY (tee hee)

Horrid Henry sat down on the sofa.

'I want to watch *Robot Rebels*,' said Henry.

'I'm watching *Nellie's Nursery*,' said Peter, sniffing.

'Stop sniffing,' said Henry.

'I can't help it, my nose is running,' said Peter.

'I'm sicker than you, and *I'm* not sniffing,' said Henry.

'I'm sicker than you,' said Peter.

'Faker.'

'Faker.'

'Liar.'

'Liar!'

'MUM!' shrieked Henry and Peter.

Mum came into the room, carrying a tray of cold drinks and two thermometers.

'Henry's being mean to me!' whined Peter.

'Peter's being mean to *me*!' whined Henry.

'If you're well enough to fight, you're well enough to go to school, Henry,' said Mum, glaring at him.

'I wasn't fighting, Peter was,' said Henry.

'Henry was,' said Peter, coughing.

Henry coughed louder.

Peter groaned.

Henry groaned louder.

'Uggghhhhh,' moaned Peter.

'Uggghhhhhhhhhh,' moaned Henry. 'It's not fair. I want to watch *Robot Rebels*.'

'I want to watch *Nellie's Nursery*,' whimpered Peter.

'Peter will choose what to watch because he's the sickest,' said Mum.

Peter, sicker than he was? As if. Well, no way was Henry's sick day going to be ruined by his horrible brother.

'I'm the sickest, Mum,' protested Henry. 'I just don't complain so much.'

Mum looked tired. She popped one thermometer into Henry's mouth and the other into Peter's.

'I'll be back in five minutes to check them,' she said. 'And I don't want to hear another peep from either of you,' she added, leaving the room.

Horrid Henry lay back weakly on the sofa with the thermometer in his mouth. He felt terrible. He touched his forehead. He was burning! His temperature must be 45!

I bet my temperature is so high the thermometer won't even have enough numbers, thought Henry. Just wait till Mum saw how ill he was. Then she'd be sorry she'd been so mean.

Perfect Peter started groaning. 'I'm going to be sick,' he gasped, taking the thermometer from his mouth and running from the room.

The moment Peter left, Henry leapt up from the sofa and checked Peter's thermometer. 39 degrees! Oh no, Peter had a temperature. Now Peter would start getting *all* the attention. Mum would make Henry fetch and carry for him. Peter might even get extra ice cream.

Something had to be done.

Quickly Henry plunged Peter's thermometer into the glass of iced water.

Beep. Beep. Horrid Henry took out his own thermometer. It read 37.5C. Normal.

Normal! His temperature was normal? That was impossible. How could his temperature be normal when he was so ill?

If Mum saw that normal temperature she'd have him dressed for school in three seconds. Obviously there was something wrong with that stupid thermometer.

Horrid Henry held it to the light bulb. Just to warm it up a little, he thought.

Clump. Clump.

Yikes! Mum was coming back.

Quickly Henry yanked Peter's thermometer out of the iced water and replaced his own in his mouth. Oww! It was hot.

'Let's see if you have a temperature,' said Mum. She took the thermometer out of Henry's mouth.

'50 degrees!' she shrieked.

Oops.

'The thermometer must be broken,' mumbled Henry. 'But I still have a temperature. I'm boiling.'

'Hmmn,' said Mum, feeling Henry's forehead.

Peter came back into the sitting room slowly. His face was ashen.

'Check *my* temperature, Mum,' said Peter. He lay back weakly on the pillows.

Mum checked Peter's thermometer.

'10 degrees!' she shrieked.

Oops, thought Horrid Henry.

'That one must be broken too,' said Henry.

He decided to change the subject fast.

'Mum, could you open the curtains please?' said Henry.

'But I want them closed,' said Peter.

'Open!'

'Closed!'

'We'll leave them closed,' said Mum.

Peter sneezed.

'Mum!' wailed Henry. 'Peter got snot all over me.'

'Mum!' wailed Peter. 'Henry's smelly.'

Horrid Henry glared at Peter.

Perfect Peter glared at Henry.

Henry whistled.

Peter hummed.

'Henry's whistling!'

'Peter's humming!'

'MUM!' they screamed. 'Make him stop!'

'That's enough!' shouted Mum. 'Go to your bedrooms, both of you!'

Henry and Peter heaved their heavy bones upstairs to their rooms.

'It's all your fault,' said Henry.

'It's yours,' said Peter.

The front door opened. Dad came in. He looked pale.

'I'm not feeling well,' said Dad. 'I'm going to bed.'

Horrid Henry was bored. Horrid Henry was fed up. What was the point of being sick if you couldn't watch TV and you couldn't play on the computer?

'I'm hungry!' complained Horrid Henry.

'I'm thirsty,' complained Perfect Peter.

'I'm achy,' complained Dad.

'My bed's too hot!' moaned Horrid Henry.

'My bed's too cold,' moaned Perfect Peter.

'My bed's too hot and too cold,' moaned Dad.

Mum ran up the stairs.

Mum ran down the stairs.

'Ice cream!' shouted Horrid Henry.

'Hot water bottle!' shouted Perfect Peter.

'More pillows!' shouted Dad.

Mum walked up the stairs.

Mum walked down the stairs.

'Toast!' shouted Henry.

'Tissues!' croaked Peter.

'Tea!' gasped Dad.

'Can you wait a minute?' said Mum. 'I need to sit down.'

'NO!' shouted Henry, Peter, and Dad.

'All right,' said Mum.

She plodded up the stairs.

She plodded down the stairs.

'My head is hurting!'

'My throat is hurting!'

'My stomach is hurting!'

Mum trudged up the stairs.

Mum trudged down the stairs.

'Crisps,' screeched Henry.

'Throat lozenge,' croaked Peter.

'Hankie,' wheezed Dad.

Mum staggered up the stairs.

Mum staggered down the stairs.

Then Horrid Henry saw the time. Three-thirty. School was finished! The weekend was here! It was amazing, thought Horrid Henry, how much better he suddenly felt.

Horrid Henry threw off his duvet and leapt out of bed.

'Mum!' he shouted. 'I'm feeling much better. Can I go and play on the computer now?'

Mum staggered into his room.

'Thank goodness you're better, Henry,' she whispered. 'I feel terrible. I'm going to bed. Could you bring me a cup of tea?'

What?

'I'm busy,' snapped Henry.

Mum glared at him.

'All right,' said Henry, grudgingly. Why couldn't Mum get her own tea? She had legs, didn't she?

Horrid Henry escaped into the sitting room. He sat down at the computer and loaded 'Intergalactic Robot Rebellion: This Time It's Personal'. Bliss. He'd zap some robots, then have a go at 'Snake Master's Revenge'.

'Henry!' gasped Mum. 'Where's my tea?'

'Henry!' rasped Dad. 'Bring me a drink of water!'

'Henry!' whimpered Peter. 'Bring me an extra blanket.'

Horrid Henry scowled. Honestly, how was he meant to concentrate with all these interruptions?

'Tea!'

'Water!'

'Blanket!'

'Get it yourself!' he howled. What was he, a servant?

'Henry!' spluttered Dad. 'Come up here this minute.'

Slowly, Horrid Henry got to his feet. He looked longingly at the flashing screen. But what choice did he have?

'I'm sick too!' shrieked Horrid Henry. 'I'm going back to bed.'

Dear Miss Battle-Axe
Henry cudn't come to school
Yesterday because a wirwolf
bit him.
Yours sincerly
Henry's mum.

Dear Mis Battle-Axe
Henry has the black plage
So he can't take his maths
test today or do P.E.
The docter says doing any
homework cud be DEADLY

Yours Sincerly
Henrys mum.

Dear Mis Battle-Axe
Henry was sik yesterday with
a temprature of 52C. He
was so hot he set fire to his
bed which burned his room wich
mant he had no clothes to wear.
Yours Sincerly
Henry's Mum

HORRID HENRY
PEEKS AT
PETER'S DIARY

'What are you doing?' demanded Horrid Henry, bursting into Peter's bedroom.

'Nothing,' said Perfect Peter quickly, slamming his notebook shut.

'Yes you are,' said Henry.

'Get out of my room,' said Peter. 'You're not allowed to come in unless I say so.'

Horrid Henry leaned over Peter's shoulder.

'What are you writing?'

'None of your business,' said Peter. He covered the closed notebook tightly with his arm.

'It is *too* my business if you're writing about *me*.'

'It's *my* diary. I can write what I want to,' said Peter. 'Miss Lovely said we should keep a diary for a week and write in it every day.'

'Bo-ring,' said Henry, yawning.

'No it isn't,' said Peter. 'Anyway, you'll find out next week what I'm writing: I've been chosen to read my diary out loud for our class assembly.'

Horrid Henry's heart turned to ice.

Peter read his diary out loud? So the whole school could hear Peter's lies about him? No way!

'Gimme that!' screamed Horrid Henry, lunging for the diary.

'No!' screamed Peter, holding on tight. 'MUUUM! Help! Henry's in my room! And he didn't knock!

And he won't leave!'

'Shut up, tattle-tale,' hissed Henry, forcing Peter's fingers off the diary.

'MUUUUMMMMMM!' shrieked Peter.

Mum stomped up the stairs.

Henry opened the diary. But before he could read a single word Mum burst in.

'He snatched my diary! And he told me to shut up!' wailed Peter.

'Henry! Stop annoying your brother,' said Mum.

'I wasn't,' said Henry.

'Yes he was,' snivelled Peter.

'And now you've made him cry,' said Mum. 'Say sorry.'

'I was just asking about his homework,' protested Henry innocently.

'He was trying to read my diary,' said Peter.

'Henry!' said Mum. 'Don't be horrid. A diary is private. Now leave your brother alone.'

It was so unfair. Why did Mum always believe Peter?

Humph. Horrid Henry stalked out of Peter's bedroom. Well, no way was Henry waiting until class assembly to find out what Peter had written.

Horrid Henry checked to the right. Horrid Henry checked to the left. Mum was downstairs working on the computer. Dad was in the garden. Peter was playing at Goody-Goody Gordon's house.

At last, the coast was clear. He'd been trying to get hold of Peter's diary for days. There was no time to lose.

Tomorrow was Peter's class assembly. Would he mention Sunday's food fight, when Henry had been forced to throw soggy pasta at Peter? Or when Henry had to push Peter off the comfy black chair and pinch him? Or yesterday when Henry banished him from the Purple Hand Club and Peter had run screaming to Mum? A lying, slimy worm like Peter

340

would be sure to make it look like Henry was the villain when in fact Peter was always to blame.

Even worse, what horrid lies had Peter been making up about him? People would read Peter's ravings and think they were true. When Henry was famous, books would be written about him, and someone would find Peter's diary and believe it! When things were written down they had a horrible way of seeming to be true even when they were big fat lies.

Henry sneaked into Peter's bedroom and shut the door. Now, where was that diary? Henry glanced at Peter's tidy desk. Peter kept it on the second shelf, next to his crayons and trophies.

The diary was gone.

Rats. Peter must have hidden it.

That little worm, thought Horrid Henry. Why on earth would he hide his diary? And *where* on earth would that smelly toad hide it? Behind his 'Good as Gold' certificates? In the laundry basket? Underneath his stamp collection?

He checked Peter's sock drawer. No diary.

He checked Peter's underwear drawer. No diary.

He peeked under Peter's pillow, and under Peter's bed. Still no diary.

OK, where would *I* hide a diary, thought Horrid Henry desperately. Easy. I'd put it in a chest and bury it in the garden, with a pirate curse on it.

Somehow he doubted Perfect Peter would be so clever.

OK, thought Henry, if I were an ugly toad like him, where would I hide it?

The bookcase. Of course. What better place to hide a book?

Henry strolled over to Peter's bookcase, with all the books arranged neatly in alphabetical order. Aha! What was that sticking out between *The Happy Nappy* and *The Hoppy Hippo*?

Gotcha, thought Horrid Henry, yanking the diary off the shelf. At last he would know Peter's secrets.

He'd make him cross out all his lies if it was the last thing he did.

Horrid Henry sat down and began to read:

<u>Monday</u>
Today I drew a picture of my teacher, Miss Lovely. Miss Lovely gave me a gold star for reading. That's because I'm the best reader in the class. And the best at maths. And the best at everything else.

<u>Tuesday</u>
Today I said please and thank you 236 times

<u>Wednesday</u>
Today I ate all my vegetables

> Thursday
> Today I sharpened my pencils.
> I ate all my sprouts and had seconds.
>
> Friday
> Today I wrote a poem to my mummy
>
> I Love my mummy,
> I came out of her tummy,
> Her food is yummy,
> She is so scrummy,
> I love my mummy.

Slowly Horrid Henry closed Peter's diary. He knew Peter's diary would be bad. But never in his worst nightmares had he imagined anything this bad.

Perfect Peter hadn't mentioned him once. Not once.

You'd think I didn't even live in this house, thought Henry. He was outraged. How dare Peter *not* write about him? And then all the stupid things Peter *had* written.

Henry's name would be mud when people heard

Peter's diary in assembly and found out what a sad brother he had. Everyone would tease him. Horrid Henry would never live down the shame.

Peter needed Henry's help, and he needed it fast. Horrid Henry grabbed a pencil and got to work.

Monday
Today I drew a picture of my teacher, Miss Lovely. I drew her with piggy ears and a grate big giant belly Then I turned it into a dartbord Miss Lovely gave me a gold star for reading. Miss Lovely is my worst teacher ever. She should reely be

called Miss Lumpy.
Miss Dumpy Lumpy is wot Gordon
and I call her behind her back.
Tee hee, she'll never know!

**I'm the best reader in the class. And
the best at maths. And the best at
everything else.** Too bad I have
smelly pants and nitty hair

That's more like it, thought Horrid Henry.

Tuesday
Today I said please and thank you
236 times

~~Toda~~ Not! I called Mum a big
blobby pants face. I called Dad
a stinky fish. Then I played
Pirats with the worlds greatest
brother, Henry. I wish I were as

clever as Henry. But I know that's imposibel.

Wednesday
Today I ate all my vegetables

then I sneeked loads of sweets from the sweet jar and lied to dad about it. I am a very good liar. No one should ever beleeve a word I say. Henry gets the blame but reely every thing is always my fault.

Thursday
Today I sharpened my pencils.

All the better to write rude notes!

I ate all my sprouts and had
Seconds. Then threw up all over
Mum. Eeugh, what a smell. I
reelly am a smelly toad. I am
so lucky to have a grate brother
like Henry. He is always so nice to me
Hip Hip Hurray for Henry

Friday
Today I wrote a poem to my Dummy
I Love my Dummy,
It's my best chummy
It tastes so yummy,
It is so scrummy,
I love my Dummy.

Much better, thought Horrid Henry. Now that's
what I call a diary. Everyone would have died of
boredom otherwise.

Henry carefully replaced Peter's diary in the bookcase. I hope Peter appreciates what I've done for him, thought Horrid Henry.

The entire school gathered in the hall for assembly. Peter's class sat proudly on benches at the front. Henry's class sat cross-legged on the floor. The parents sat on chairs down both sides.

Mum and Dad waved at Peter. He waved shyly back.

Miss Lovely stood up.

'Hello Mums and Dads, boys and girls, welcome to our class assembly. This term our class has been keeping diaries. We're going to read some of them to you now. First to read will be Peter. Everyone pay attention, and see if you too can be as good as I know Peter has been. I'd like everyone here to copy one of Peter's good deeds. I know I can't wait to hear how he has spent this last week.'

Peter stood up, and opened his diary. In a big loud voice, he read:

MONDAY

'Today I drew a picture of my teacher, Miss Lovely.' Peter glanced up at Miss Lovely. She beamed at him.

'I drew her with piggy ears and a great big giant belly. Then I turned it into a dartboard.'

What??! It was always difficult to read out loud and understand what he had read, but something didn't sound right. He didn't remember writing about a pig with a big belly. Nervously Peter looked up at Mum and Dad. Was he imagining it, or did their smiles seem more like frowns? Peter shook his head, and carried on.

'Miss Lovely gave me a gold star for reading.'

Phew, that was better! He must have misheard himself before.

'Miss Lovely is my worst teacher ever. She should really be called Miss Lumpy. Miss Dumpy Lumpy—'

'Thank you, that's quite enough,' interrupted Miss Lovely sternly, as the school erupted in shrieks of laughter. Her face was pink. 'Peter, see me after assembly. Ted will now tell us all about skeletons.'

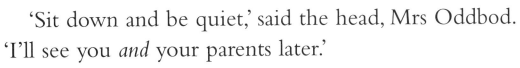

'But—but—' gasped Perfect Peter. 'I—I didn't, I never—'

'Sit down and be quiet,' said the head, Mrs Oddbod. 'I'll see you *and* your parents later.'

'WAAAAAAAAAAA!' wailed Peter.

Mum and Dad stared at their feet. Why had they ever had children? Where was a trapdoor when you needed one?

'Waaaaaaaa,' whimpered Mum and Dad.

Naturally, Henry got into trouble. Big big trouble. It was so unfair. Why didn't anyone believe him when he said he'd improved Peter's diary for his own good? Honestly, he would never *ever* do Peter a favour again.

HORRID HENRY'S DIARY

MONDAY Today I wrot Magaret a pome. I can't beleeve she didn't like it (tee hee). I surped ~~Peters~~ 5 chips off Peters plate when he wasn't looking, and sneaked all my peas on to his !!!

TUESDAY Today I hid a Mad Max comick inside my maths book during class. Unfortunately, I forgot to check that my maths book was the rite way up — Woops! ∞∞∞

WEDNESDAY Great day! I found 50p on the street and bougt a huge bar of chocolit !!!

THURSDAY Mum wouldn't let me wach extra T.V. so I called her a stinky fish. Well she is. Then Dad wouldn't let me have more crisps, so I called him a big blobby pants face delux. Now I am in my room.

FRIDAY Peter tried to grab the cumfy black chair but I tricked him by telling him that Mum was calling him. Then I nabbed it. A perfick start to the weekend !!!

HORRID HENRY'S CHRISTMAS PLAY

A Cold Dark Day in November
(37 days till Christmas)

Horrid Henry slumped on the carpet and willed the clock to go faster. Only five more minutes to hometime! Already Henry could taste those crisps he'd be sneaking from the cupboard.

Miss Battle-Axe droned on about school dinners (yuck), the new drinking fountain blah blah blah, maths homework blah blah blah, the school Christmas play blah blah . . . what? Did Miss Battle-Axe say . . . Christmas play? Horrid Henry sat up.

'This is a brand-new play with singing and dancing,' continued Miss Battle-Axe. 'And both the older and the younger children are taking part this year.'

Singing! Dancing! Showing off in front of the whole school! Years ago, when Henry was in the infants' class, he'd played eighth sheep in the nativity play and had snatched the baby from the manger and refused to hand him back. Henry hoped Miss Battle-Axe wouldn't remember.

Because Henry had to play the lead. He had to. Who else but Henry could be an all-singing, all-dancing Joseph?

'I want to be Mary,' shouted every girl in the class.

'I want to be a wise man!' shouted Rude Ralph.

'I want to be a sheep!' shouted Anxious Andrew.

'I want to be Joseph!' shouted Horrid Henry.

'No, me!' shouted Jazzy Jim.

'Me!' shouted Brainy Brian.

'Quiet!' shrieked Miss Battle-Axe. 'I'm the director, and my decision about who will act which part is final. I've cast the play as follows: Margaret. You will be Mary.' She handed her a thick script.

Moody Margaret whooped with joy. All the other girls glared at her.

'Susan, front legs of the donkey; Linda, hind legs; cows, Fiona and Clare. Blades of grass—' Miss Battle-Axe continued assigning parts.

Pick me for Joseph, pick me for Joseph, Horrid Henry begged silently. Who better than the best actor in the school to play the starring part?

'I'm a sheep, I'm a sheep, I'm a beautiful sheep!' warbled Singing Soraya.

'I'm a shepherd!' beamed Jolly Josh.

'I'm an angel,' trilled Magic Martha.

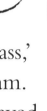

'I'm a blade of grass,' sobbed Weepy William.

'Joseph will be played by—'

'ME!' screamed Henry.

'Me!' screamed New Nick, Greedy Graham, Dizzy Dave and Aerobic Al.

'—Peter,' said Miss Battle-Axe. 'From Miss Lovely's class.'

Horrid Henry felt as if he'd been slugged in the stomach. Perfect Peter? His *younger* brother? Perfect Peter get the starring part?

'It's not fair!' howled Horrid Henry.

Miss Battle-Axe glared at him.

'Henry, you're—' Miss Battle-Axe consulted her list. Please not a blade of grass, please not a blade of grass, prayed Horrid Henry, shrinking. That would be just like Miss Battle-Axe, to humiliate him. Anything but that—

'—the innkeeper.'

The innkeeper! Horrid Henry sat up, beaming. How stupid he'd been: the *innkeeper* must be the starring part. Henry could see himself now, polishing glasses, throwing darts, pouring out big foaming Fizzywizz drinks to all his happy customers while singing a song about the joys of innkeeping. Then he'd get into a nice long argument about why there was no room at the inn, and finally, the chance to slam the door in Moody Margaret's face after he'd pushed her away. Wow. Maybe he'd even get a second song. 'Ten Green Bottles' would fit right into the story: he'd sing and dance while knocking his less talented classmates off a wall. Wouldn't that be fun!

Miss Battle-Axe handed a page to Henry. 'Your script,' she said.

Henry was puzzled. Surely there were some pages missing?

He read:

(Joseph knocks. The innkeeper opens the door.)

JOSEPH: Is there any room at the inn?
INNKEEPER: No.

(The innkeeper shuts the door.)

Horrid Henry turned over the page.

It was blank. He held it up to the light.

There was no secret writing. That was it.

His entire part was one line. One stupid puny line. Not even a line, a word. 'No.'

Where was his song? Where was his dance with the bottles and the guests at the inn? How could he, Horrid Henry, the best actor in the class (and indeed, the world) be given just one word in the school play? Even the donkeys got a song.

Worse, after he said his *one* word, Perfect Peter and Moody Margaret got to yack for hours about mangers and wise men and shepherds and sheep, and then sing a duet, while he, Henry, hung about behind the hay with the blades of grass.

It was so unfair!

He should be the star of the show, not his stupid worm of a brother. Why on earth was Peter cast as

Joseph anyway? He was a terrible actor. He couldn't sing, he just squeaked like a squished toad. And why was Margaret playing Mary? Now she'd never stop bragging and swaggering.

'Isn't it exciting!' said Mum.

'Isn't it thrilling!' said Dad. 'Our little boy, the star of the show.'

'Well done, Peter,' said Mum.

'We're so proud of you,' said Dad.

Perfect Peter smiled modestly.

'Of course I'm not *really* the star,' he said, 'Everyone's important, even little parts like the blades of grass and the innkeeper.'

Horrid Henry pounced. He was a Great White shark lunging for the kill.

squealed Peter. 'Henry bit me!'

'Henry! Don't be horrid!' snapped Mum.

'Henry! Go to your room!' snapped Dad.

Horrid Henry stomped upstairs and slammed the door. How could he bear the humiliation of playing the innkeeper when Peter was the star? He'd just have to force Peter to switch roles with him. Henry was sure he could find a way to persuade Peter, but persuading Miss Battle-Axe was a different matter. Miss Battle-Axe had a mean, horrible way of never doing what Henry wanted.

Maybe he could trick Peter into leaving the show. Yes! And then nobly offer to replace him.

But unfortunately, there was no guarantee Miss Battle-Axe would give Henry Peter's role. She'd probably just replace Peter with Goody-Goody Gordon. He was stuck.

And then Horrid Henry had a brilliant, spectacular idea. Why hadn't he thought of this before? If he couldn't play a bigger part, he'd just have to make his part bigger. For instance, he could *scream* 'No.' *That* would get a reaction. Or he could bellow 'No,' and then hit Joseph. I'm an angry innkeeper, thought Horrid Henry, and I hate guests coming to my inn. Certainly smelly ones like Joseph. Or he could shout 'No!', hit Joseph, then rob him. I'm a robber innkeeper, thought Henry. Or, I'm a robber *pretending* to be an innkeeper. That would liven up the play a bit. Maybe he could be a French robber innkeeper, shout '*Non*', and rob Mary and Joseph. Or he was a French robber *pirate* innkeeper, so he could shout '*Non*,' tie Mary and Joseph up and make them walk the plank. Hmmm, thought Horrid Henry. Maybe my part won't be so small. After all, the innkeeper *was* the most important character.

12 DECEMBER
(only 13 more days till Christmas)

Rehearsals had been going on forever. Horrid Henry spent most of his time slumping in a chair. He'd never seen such a boring play. Naturally he'd done everything he could to improve it.

'Can't I add a dance?' asked Henry.

'No,' snapped Miss Battle-Axe.

'Can't I add a teeny-weeny little song?' Henry pleaded.

'No!' said Miss Battle-Axe.

'But how does the innkeeper *know* there's no room?' said Henry. 'I think I should—'

Miss Battle-Axe glared at him with her red eyes.

'One more word from you, Henry, and you'll change places with Linda,' snapped Miss Battle-Axe. 'Blades of grass, let's try again . . .'

Eeek! An innkeeper with one word was infinitely better than being invisible as the hind legs of a donkey. Still—it was so unfair. He was only trying to help.

22 DECEMBER
(only 3 more days till Christmas!)

Showtime! Not a teatowel was to be found in any local shop. Mums and dads had been up all night frantically sewing costumes. Now the waiting and the rehearsing were over.

Everyone lined up on stage behind the curtain. Peter and Margaret waited on the side to make their big entrance as Mary and Joseph.

'Isn't it exciting, Henry, being in a real play?' whispered Peter.

'NO,' snarled Henry.

'Places, everyone, for the opening song,' hissed Miss Battle-Axe. 'Now remember, don't worry if you make a little mistake: just carry on and no one will notice.'

'But I still think I should have an argument with

Mary and Joseph about whether there's room,' said Henry. 'Shouldn't I at least check to see—'

'No!' snapped Miss Battle-Axe, glaring at him. 'If I hear another peep from you, Henry, you will sit behind the bales of hay and Jim will play your part. Blades of grass! Line up with the donkeys! Sheep! Get ready to baaa . . . Bert! Are you a sheep or a blade of grass?'

'I dunno,' said Beefy Bert.

Mrs Oddbod went to the front of the stage. 'Welcome everyone, mums and dads, boys and girls, to our new Christmas play, a little different from previous years. We hope you all enjoy a brand new show!'

Miss Battle-Axe started the CD player. The music pealed. The curtain rose. The audience stamped and cheered. Stars twinkled. Cows mooed. Horses neighed. Sheep baa'ed. Cameras flashed.

Horrid Henry stood in the wings and watched the shepherds do their Highland dance. He still hadn't decided for sure how he was going to play his part. There were so many possibilities. It was so hard to choose.

Finally, Henry's big moment arrived.

He strode across the stage and waited behind the closed inn door for Mary and Joseph.

367

Knock! **Knock! Knock!**

The innkeeper stepped forward and opened the door. There was Moody Margaret, simpering away as Mary, and Perfect Peter looking full of himself as Joseph.

'Is there any room at the inn?' asked Joseph.

Good question, thought Horrid Henry. His mind was blank. He'd thought of so many great things he *could* say that what he was *supposed* to say had just gone straight out of his head.

'Is there any room at the inn?' repeated Joseph loudly.

'Yes,' said the innkeeper. 'Come on in.'

Joseph looked at Mary.

Mary looked at Joseph.

The audience murmured.

Oops, thought Horrid Henry. Now he remembered. He'd been supposed to say no. Oh well, in for a penny, in for a pound.

The innkeeper grabbed Mary and Joseph's sleeves and yanked them through the door. 'Come on in, I haven't got all day.'

' . . . but . . . but . . . the inn's *full*,' said Mary.

'No it isn't,' said the innkeeper.

'Is too.'

'Is not. It's my inn and I should know. This is the best inn in Bethlehem, we've got TVs and beds, and—' the innkeeper paused for a moment. What *did* inns have in them? '—and computers!'

Mary glared at the innkeeper.

The innkeeper glared at Mary.

Miss Battle-Axe gestured frantically from the wings.

'This inn looks full to me,' said Mary firmly. 'Come on Joseph, let's go to the stable.'

'Oh, don't go there, you'll get fleas,' said the innkeeper.

'So?' said Mary.

'I love fleas,' said Joseph weakly.

'And it's full of manure.'

'So are you,' snapped Mary.

'Don't be horrid, Mary,' said the innkeeper severely. 'Now sit down and rest your weary bones and I'll sing you a song.' And the innkeeper started singing:

'Ten green bottles, standing on a wall
Ten green bottles, standing on a wall,
And if one green bottle should accidentally
    fall—

'Ooohhh!'

moaned Mary. 'I'm having the baby.'

'Can't you wait till I've finished my song?' snapped the inkeeper.

'NO!' bellowed Mary.

Miss Battle-Axe drew her hand across her throat.

Henry ignored her. After all, the show must go on.

'Come on, Joseph,' interrupted Mary. 'We're going to the stable.'

'OK,' said Joseph.

'You're making a big mistake,' said the innkeeper. 'We've got satellite TV and . . .'

Miss Battle-Axe ran on stage and nabbed him.

'Thank you, innkeeper, your other guests need you now,' said Miss Battle-Axe, grabbing him by the collar.

'Merry Christmas!' shrieked Horrid Henry as she
yanked him off-stage.

There was a very long silence.

'Bravo!' yelled Moody Margaret's deaf aunt.

Mum and Dad weren't sure what to do. Should
they clap, or run away to a place where no one knew
them?

Mum clapped.

Dad hid his face in his hands.

'Do you think anyone noticed?' whispered Mum.

Dad looked at Mrs Oddbod's grim face. He sank down in his chair. Maybe one day he would learn how to make himself invisible.

'But what was I *supposed* to do?' said Horrid Henry afterwards in Mrs Oddbod's office. 'It's not *my* fault I forgot my line. Miss Battle-Axe said not to worry if we made a mistake and just to carry on.'

Could he help it if a star was born?

372

KING HENRY THE HORRIBLE'S FACT FILE

Worst subjects

Miss Battle-Axe

Moody Margaret
Stuck-up Steve
Perfect Peter
Mrs Oddbod

Best banquet

To start:
Chocolate
    yum-yums

Main courses:
Pizza
Burgers
Chips
Chocolate

Desserts:
Chocolate ice cream
Chocolate cake
Chocolate biscuits
Fudge

Worst banquet

Chef had his head chopped off

To start: Spinach tart

Main courses:

Mussels
Tripe

Brussels sprouts
Cauliflower

Dessert:
Fresh fruit

Ugh!

Best punishments

Piranha-infested moat
Snakepit
Man-eating crocodiles
Scorpion cage

Best law

Parents have to go to school, not children

Worst crimes

Saying the word 'chores'
Setting homework
Bedtime

Best throne

Comfy black chair

Worst throne

School chair

Best regal robes

Terminator Gladiator
dressing-gown

Worst regal robes

Pageboy outfit

Best palace

300 rooms with 300 TVs

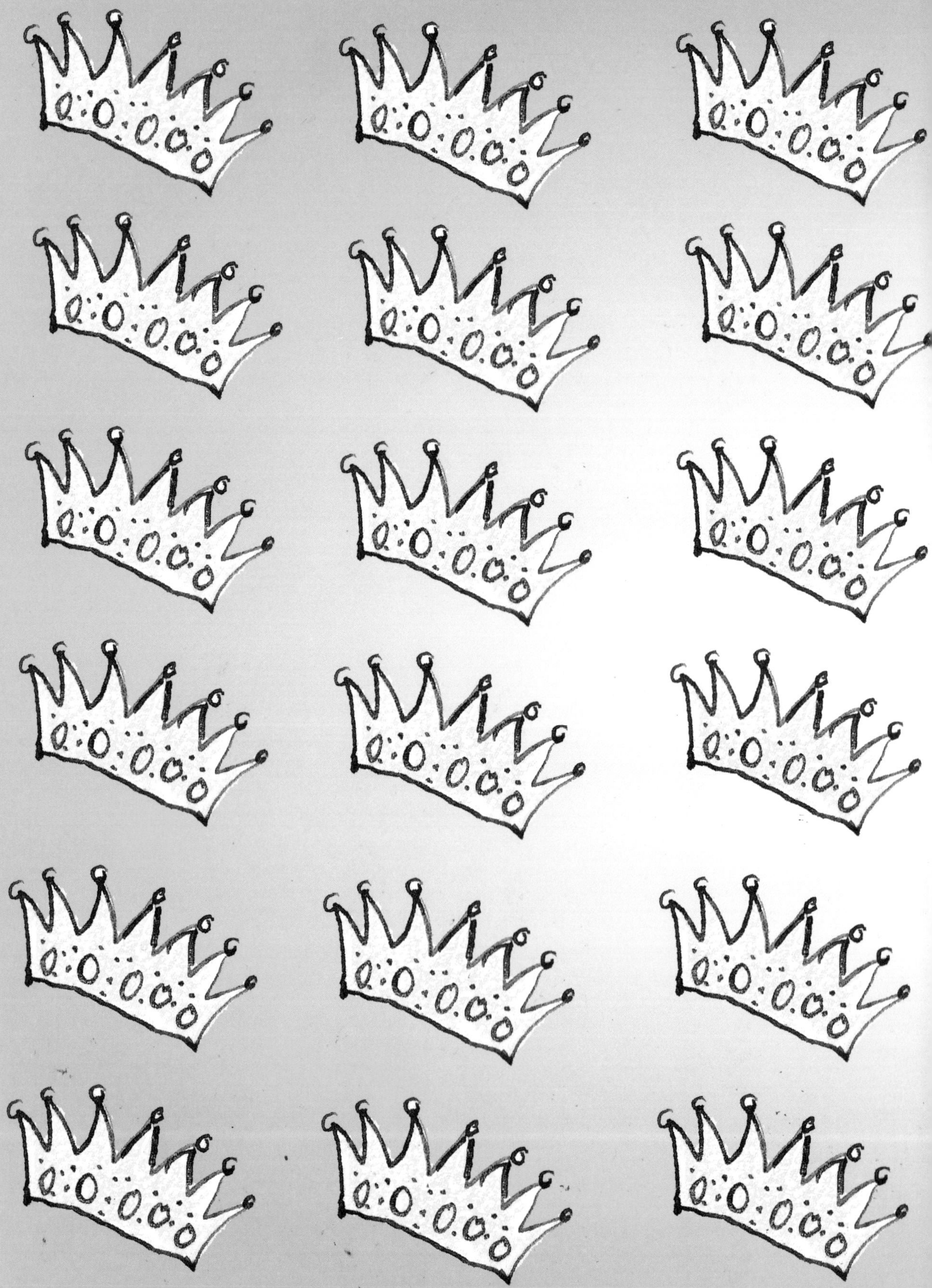